LOVE HATE LAW

A Kramer-O'Hara Legal Romance

By:

MARK M. BELLO

10 Grand Publications

4301 Orchard Lake Road

Suite 180-124

West Bloomfield, MI 48323

ISBN-: EBook ISBN 978-1-956595-18-5

Print   ISBN 978-1-956595-19-2

TABLE OF CONTENTS

PROLOGUE

THE INSURRECTION

Rinke

Capitol Park was a canopy of color. Trees, yet to shed leaves for the winter, treated visitors to a stunning array of reds, purples, oranges, and golds. Pockets of morning dew caught beneath the pine boughs, heavy with seedling cones, fanned out their intoxicating scent on the fingers of an erratic breeze.

On this fall day in Lansing, Michigan, soon-to-be-former governor Gordon Rinke stepped to the podium. The election was over—a clear and convincing victory for the newly elected governor, Charlie Page. Deeply divided Michigan would now head in a different direction.

Not so fast, declared Rinke. In a stunning display of narcissism and political arrogance, Rinke refused to concede. "They rigged the count," he cried, making camera-grabbing protests.

He rallied his supporters, appealing to the lowest common denominator. His most significant financial contributor was Brandon North, founding member of the Michigan Watch Patrol, a far-right militia group preparing for a second American revolution or civil war. The Patrol was pro-gun and anti-government, opposed to Michigan's COVID-19 vaccination and lockdown protocol, and part of a mini-rebellion that helped sweep Gordon Rinke into office.

For weeks, Rinke encouraged followers like North to descend on the Capitol, protest the outcome, prevent certification of the vote, demand a recount, declare the election fraudulent, and induce a duly appointed legislative committee to overturn the results.

Rinke squinted in the bright sunlight, gazing at the 'magnificent turnout,' buoyed that his last-ditch ploy might work. *Is the impossible possible?* He marveled at his supporters' ignorant obedience. *If I told these guys to kidnap Page, they'd do it!*

Like a preacher, Rinke raised his arms to the sky, requesting silence. The crowd obeyed. *Remarkable!* He gazed at his supporters, some dressed in combat gear, many armed, perhaps dangerous. They could become violent, but not toward him or his people. *Who cares? These Capitol frauds certainly don't care about me!*

Police were scattered among the protestors, sticking out like sore thumbs, deeply concerned that this 'rally for justice' might turn violent. The protestors might turn their aggression toward contrary reporters or the police. Lansing and Michigan State Police were vastly outnumbered. The National Guard was on standby.

"My fellow Michiganders," Rinke began. The crowd went wild at the sound of his voice. "I come before you today for one reason only—to save Michigan. This election was not legitimate! We have a rigged system!"

The crowd roared, "bullshit, not legit." Rinke silenced the audience with a raised arm.

"Look at this crowd!" he shouted. "The media will not accurately report the size of this crowd." He gestured to camera operators to turn their cameras to the decent-sized crowd, but they refused to do his bidding. "Cowards and traitors, the lot of you," he scowled.

"The media is our state's biggest problem—fake news, everywhere!" The crowd chanted "fake news" until Rinke ordered them to stop.

"Will we stand back and see our victory stolen by our opponents?"

"Hell no!" His followers cried.

"We will rise up and declare that we're mad as hell and will not take it anymore!" Rinke borrowed the famous line from *Network*.

"This election was not even close!" His first honest remark of the day—he did not mean it as a concession to Page's margin of victory.

"We will march to the Capitol, take back our State, and restore integrity to our elections. I will lead you into the people's building. If we must fight, we will fight like hell! Break down doors and force your way in if you must. Drain the swamp and trample anyone in our way. Let's take back our Capitol!"

Rinke railed on far too long, for more than an hour. The speech finally ended, and his security team swept him away. Cheering supporters rushed toward the Capitol, chanting, "Stop the steal." State and Lansing police erected a barricade at the top of the Capitol steps and formed a defensive line on the center steps leading to the building.

As the speech droned on, a small group of Watch Patrol members gathered at the lightly guarded back entrances on the other side of the building. They quickly breached the building. Armed with assault rifles, these protestors raced through the lobby and headed toward the front entrance. When they reached their destination, they poured through the panic doors toward the line of officers. They kicked the barriers down the stairs.

Each member selected an officer, barreled into them from behind, and sent the officers tumbling down the long Capitol stairway. At the same time, Brandon North and a second group of rioters ascended the stairway and watched helpless, injured officers roll past them down the stairs. Patrol members breached the main entrance and stampeded over anyone in their path. After their tumble down the stairs, uninjured or slightly injured officers resumed upright positions and gave chase up the stairs. Legislators had quietly evacuated the Capitol *before* the breach—senators and state representatives were never in danger.

Three more hours passed before Capitol officers declared the building secure. Governor Rinke, who inspired the riot and promised to lead protestors into the Capitol, had disappeared. In the aftermath of the insurrection, this beautiful beacon of law and justice suffered millions in property and precious artifact damage. Several officers and citizens were injured—one citizen, a young legislative assistant, was trampled to death by the stampeding mob at the front entrance.

At a private, secure location a few blocks from the Capitol, the final vote certification declared Charlie Page the winner by a wide margin. The violence was for naught. Michigan had a new governor.

CHAPTER ONE

TWO MONTHS LATER

Andrea

Can someone love a career choice and hate it at the same time? Andrea Kramer was glad she went to law school and proud to graduate summa cum laude from the University of Michigan. She took school seriously—her activist parents would not have it any other way. Their activism rubbed off. While she wasn't always successful in her endeavors, it wasn't for lack of trying.

She sat in a small booth at the *Coffee Mug Café*, waiting for Mary Beth to take her order and, more importantly, pour her precious coffee. The café was known for its coffee, but Mary Beth's fantastic chocolate doughnuts brought her in that morning. Andrea was tense. Today, she celebrated the official opening of her new law office—celebrations required chocolate.

"A couple dozen of your chocolate doughnuts and a thermos filled with coffee, please?" She called out to Mary Beth, who busily slapped mugs and plates on the counter for a line of customers.

"Oh, and that's to go," she added. Law school and a short, so far uninspiring career in the law taught her to be careful with her words. She left nothing to chance. No lawyer wants to leave matters to a jury or a judge so they may draw their own conclusions. Good lawyers, like directors of award-winning movies, *directed* conclusions.

"Today, you leave the door unlocked, huh?" Mary Beth teased. "Well, it's about time. Nobody can hire you if you don't let them in . . . or maybe that's the idea?"

She tipped forward from her rubber band waist. Her practiced aim refilled Andrea's cup from two feet overhead. Like a bartender who practiced glass acrobatics, Mary Beth's steady aim resulted from a generation's worth of waiting tables. She knew her business *and* customers, the primary reason she was Andrea's favorite.

Andrea dragged herself in for a pick-me-up each morning before heading to Ann Arbor. Today, she'd stay in Saline. Dressed for painting, a scarf tied around her reddish brunette hair, not a speck of make-up was wasted. Andrea hoped to finish renovating a historic home into the Law Offices of Andrea Kramer.

The office was a unique conversion. Several years earlier, an architect converted a grain silo and barn into a modern residence. Shortly after the Dupree family moved into the home, all five family members were murdered, execution style. The murder was never solved.

A few years later, a family from out of town bought the place, then quickly abandoned it after experiencing what they called *paranormal* activity. The new owners swore, up and down, that the house had a strange smell—like something had died. The children claimed to have observed three shadowy forms in their bedroom. Presumably, these were the Dupree children.

An investor purchased the home cheaply, converted the zoning, and listed it as a professional office. The property sat vacant for years—everyone in town knew the history.

Andrea was not superstitious. Besides, the price was right, and the conversion was intriguing. The silo had circular shelving for potential use as a working law library or file room. The barn was spacious and had a vaulted hardwood ceiling. Andrea envisioned rental offices and a beautiful conference room. The home had a kitchen, living room, three bedrooms, and a sunroom. The living room would be a waiting area, reception, and secretarial space. The bedrooms would be attorney offices, and the sunroom would be Andrea's getaway room.

Andrea loved the place but knew better than to exhibit her enthusiasm. She wrinkled her nose as Meagan Fields, an old college chum, walked her through.

"Any way to get rid of that odor?" Andrea inquired.

"I don't smell anything."

"Smells like something or someone died."

"That's the legend, but we both know it's a bunch of malarky."

"I smell something."

Meagan grunted. "Everyone who knows the history of this place 'smells something.'" She finger-signed the quotes. "If this place had no history, the rent would quadruple. We both know that."

"I don't know. It might be difficult to get staff or clients to come into the office."

Meagan shrugged. "History or no history, this is the only building in your price range. The good news is that you lock in the rate for three years."

"I saw a local documentary about the Dupree murders. People believe it's still haunted. I don't know—"

"Jesus, Andi. Please give it a rest! I'm trying to work with you here."

"Ask them to drop the rent by a few hundred, and I'll take it. Maybe I'll embrace the history. How does Kramer Law Offices at Tranquility Manor sound?"

"Wonderful." Meagan rolled her eyes. "I'll relay your offer."

"Make it five hundred."

"Five hundred what?"

"Ask for a five-hundred-dollar reduction. No rent increases for the entire lease term and an option to renew for another three years at the same rate."

"Such a lawyer—everything's a negotiation. I'll relay the message. Anything else? Do you want the guy to pay your employees? Handle your overhead?" Meagan chided.

"He could throw in utilities and paint the place," Andrea floated.

"Don't push it, Kramer. You can pay the utilities with the five-hundred-dollar discount."

"Are you saying it's a deal?"

"I'll make it work. This guy is desperate. Don't tell anyone, but I like you better than him."

"Thanks."

"This is exciting, career-wise."

"We'll see. I'm glad to be home. Looking forward to helping real people."

After she graduated from law school, Andrea spent a few years doing corporate defense work, making rich corporate types richer and helping insurance companies deny legitimate claims. She was well-paid but miserable. She hated screwing people. Without notice, she walked into the senior partner's office one day and quit.

Andrea still felt unfulfilled a year after renting an office from a small personal injury firm, doing the firm's overflow district court work, and covering scheduling conflicts. She welcomed a return to her hometown and the opportunity to help people in her community.

Meagan interrupted her thoughts.

"How's life treating you? Any interesting prospects?"

"Prospects?"

"Come on, Andi, spill. How's your love life?"

"Not everyone can be as lucky as you. Jason is quite the rising star."

"He's *too* focused on his career for my taste."

"Poor baby. Are you being ignored?" Andrea teased.

"A woman has certain desires, you know. He satisfies most of them. Look at you, the big-shot lawyer changing the subject. The question was about *your* love life, missy, not mine."

"Nothing to report, I'm afraid. Maybe after I get my office going."

"The good ones will all be taken."

"Love will come—I'm not going to force it."

"The famous last words of an old maid."

"That's a stretch—don't you think? I'm still in my twenties."

"Close to thirty."

Andrea signed the lease the next day. The landlord eyed her. "New law practice, eh? Are you sure you'll be able to make the rent?"

Andi pivoted her head to face him. "You have other takers?" She sniffed the air. "What's that smell?"

"Huh?" He grumbled and sniffed at the air. "I don't smell anything."

"Everyone else does."

"Rent is due first of the month, *every* month. Don't let me down," he warned.

"You'll get your money." She felt her temper begin to flare, and for good reason. The landlord had a nightmare on his hands and refused to admit it. In the end, he made quite a show of conciliation and left. Andrea changed the locks that same day and began sprucing the place up, making the place look like the office she envisioned.

Everything up to that point had been without risk, without penalty. She knew things would soon change. She lingered, giving the walls an extra coat, waiting for the right area rug to cover defects in the tiled floor.

Someday, these floors will be solid wood. I'll need a tax shelter and someone to share my good fortune.

After opening the office door on her first day in business, Andrea sniffed the air and smelled only fresh paint and coffee. She placed the coffee and donuts in the corner of the reception area and glanced around, proud of her work. She walked over to what would soon be a receptionist's desk and typed a password into the computer, *DEFENSELAWYERSSUCK!*

Behind her, the front door opened. Andrea stiffened. *A client?* The moment arrived sooner than she expected.

"You the lawyer?" An older man stood in her doorway, staring at her, looking around for the receptionist or secretary who did not exist. *That will come later,* Andrea told herself.

The man wiped his hand against the thigh of his jeans, then briefly took Andrea's in the limp way a man does when confronted with the delicacy of a female hand.

"I like what you've done with the place. It's haunted, you know."

"So, I've been told. How may I help you, sir? Let's start with your name."

"I'm Arthur Longbow." He held a weathered Detroit Tigers baseball cap between roughened fingers. Every few seconds, he snuffed loudly and cleared his throat. It was a raw sound. Tears formed in his eyes.

"My daughter was at the Capitol two months ago," he whispered.

CHAPTER TWO

Michael

"What the hell?" Michael O'Hara's cell phone alarm chirped loudly enough to awaken him, ending a wonderful dream he could not quite remember. He pried his eyes open and looked around the unfamiliar room.

"Shit!" He grumbled. "Where am I?" He squirmed to the side of the bed, let his feet touch the floor, and felt a wave of dizziness and nausea as he willed his body to an upright position. That's when he saw her. A beautiful naked woman lay on top of the sheets on the opposite side of the bed.

Who the hell are you? What happened last night?

"Are you alive?" He gasped. "How could you not have heard that insidious alarm?"

He walked over to the other side and gently tapped the woman on her bare shoulder. She stirred.

Thank God! Not dead. She's got a terrific ass.

He grabbed both shoulders and shook her a bit more vigorously. She stirred, rolled onto her back, moaned, and opened her eyes.

"Morning . . . uh . . . Michael? What time is it?"

She knows my name. He studied her face and body, still trying to remember. *Who are you, beautiful? Where am I?*

He returned to his side of the bed to retrieve his cell phone. *What time is it?* He pressed a button. The screen came to life, displaying the time: nine-fifteen in the morning.

"Shit, I'm late!" He scanned the room, trying to recall *something* from the night before. His eyes settled on the bed and the naked woman. She caught him looking, stretched enthusiastically, and opened her legs. Michael sucked in a breath and paused to enjoy the view.

"Who are you? Where are we?"

"Don't you remember, darling? I'm Trudy."

Michael continued to stare at the beautiful stranger.

"We met last night at Jacoby's," she continued. "You *did* have a lot to drink."

"Jacoby's? It *is* one of my favorite places." He struggled to recall the meet.

"I was sitting at the bar, waiting for my date. You snooze, you lose, right?" she recalled.

"Huh?"

"My date was late. You were alone and transmitting vibes."

"Vibes?"

"Yeah, you know . . . vibes, like you were looking for company. You are quite a handsome man."

"Thank you. And you're a beautiful woman. I'm sure you know that." He forced a smile, still clueless.

"You moved over a few seats and introduced yourself, remember?"

"Honestly, I wish I did. How much did we have to drink?"

"Let me put it this way. You were very generous. Neither of us could drive at closing time, so you booked a room at the Greektown Hotel."

"And?"

"And what? We took an Uber to the hotel, and the rest is history. Last night was amazing!"

"I see . . . uh . . . Trudy . . . I'm beginning to remember now," he lied. "Last night was the best I've had in a long time." He glanced at his phone again.

"Listen . . . uh . . . I'm sorry to do this to you. I'm late for work. I've got to take a quick shower and run. You're welcome to stay a while if you'd like. I'll call you."

"You don't have my number."

"There's a notepad on the desk over there," he pointed. "Write it down, and I'll give you a buzz."

"You're lying. You don't remember a thing, do you?"

"I remember getting smashed," he confessed. "Not much else, I'm afraid."

"That's too bad. That *was* the best sex I've had in years. Mind-blowing!"

"I'm pleased you had a good time. I'm sure I did, too. I'd like to do this again, perhaps without the booze—"

"And the drugs."

"And the drugs." *What drugs?* "Please . . . I would love to continue this conversation. Perhaps we can meet again. Maybe get to know each other? But I am extremely late for work. Do you understand?"

"I do." The woman stretched provocatively. Michael tensed and turned. She reached out and grabbed his hand, turning him back towards her.

"I see I got your attention . . . again," she observed with a smile.

Michael pulled his hand away and looked down, embarrassed. "I've got to hit the shower. Again, stay for as long as you wish—order room service. And, please, leave your number. I'll call you."

"You're lying. You won't call, will you?"

"Why wouldn't I call? Look at you!" He continued to stare.

His phone rang, a different ringtone than the one that woke him. He answered the phone.

"Where the hell are you, Michael? Taggert is about to have a coronary." Deborah Thomas had been Michael's legal secretary since he became an associate at the Taggert firm.

"I'm just down the street." He dashed into the bathroom and turned on the shower.

"Did you just now turn on a shower?" Deb had excellent hearing.

"No," he lied. "I'm washing my hands in the sink."

"What sink? Where? You're lying, Michael. I know the difference between a shower and a sink. I'll cover for you. Just tell me where you are."

Michael hated lying to Deb. And she *always* covered for him. But these circumstances were too embarrassing. "Can we discuss it later? I'm nearby. Want me to bring you anything? Coffee? Danish?"

"Just get your ass in here. What would you do without me?"

"I refuse to even think about that possibility. I'll be there soon. Cover for me. There's dinner in it for you," he promised.

"And after dinner, my white knight?" Deb was between boyfriends. She'd been playfully flirting with the boss for years.

Michael was accustomed to the playful banter. He usually enjoyed and participated in it, but not this time. "You know my rule. No dates inside the gates."

"I quit," she kibitzed.

"You can't. I refuse to go on without you. I'll kill myself."

"Finish your shower and get the hell in here."

"You're the best."

"Yada, yada."

Michael showered and dressed in less than five minutes. Trudy still sat naked on top of the sheets. She saw Michael and parted her legs again. Michael stopped to look. Trudy seemed to revel in his body's reaction.

"Did you write down the number?" Michael turned away.

"I did, lover. Come and get it." She popped the note between her teeth.

"Please? I'm so late. I'm going to get fired." He turned back for a final look.

She frowned. He shrugged, walked to the bed, leaned over, and tried to grab the note with his teeth. She pulled him down and kissed him, which wetted and crumbled the note.

"You're a great kisser, baby," she called after him as he grabbed the note and ran out the door.

***

Michael pushed through the elevator doors at the sound of the familiar ding and swept into the law firm's lobby. The floor-length windows behind the receptionist framed a view of clouds so close a window washer could have touched them. It was the 36th floor—the named partners were Taggert, Miles & Freeman. However, Michael was the attorney currently creating firm buzz.

He was, by far, the firm's best litigator. A hot streak placed him on the partner track. As named partner, he'd earn a company Beemer, a key to the executive lounge and sports club, and a coveted country club membership. Michael could *taste* it. Once a sought-after litigator, his streak was cooled by recent trial losses and large settlements. Michael considered this a temporary aberration. What about the partners?

Michael jaunted through the hallway, entered his private office, walked to the opposite side, and opened the door separating his office from Deb's cubicle. Walking up to Deb, he leaned down from his 6'4" height and placed a key fob on the counter.

"Deb, thank you. You're a lifesaver. What do I have today?"

Deb raised her hand to halt Michael's forward movement. "Aside from your meeting with Taggert, you're clear until the six-thirty dinner. Vicki called to say the key would be at the front desk. You turned off your phone again?"

With the fluid movement of a trained athlete, Michael returned to his office and slammed the glass door.

Michael O'Hara preferred to keep his private life private. He loved Deb but didn't share intimate details of his love life with anyone. He'd been seeing Vicki for two months and vowed to remain sober throughout the evening.

"Michael? We've been waiting." He turned to see Stu Taggert, founding partner of the firm, standing outside his door.

Michael instantly put on a smile. "Stu, sorry. I got here as soon as I could. What can I do for you? Let me grab a coffee, and I'll be right over," he chirped. *Is this the day?* The entire office had been anticipating Michael's elevation to partner. He turned to grab his coffee.

"Leave it. Bring your laptop. This is a business, not a party," Stu growled. Most mornings, Stu played nine holes at the club's premier golf course and waltzed into the office with a sunny disposition.

Michael's smile wilted in place. He carefully pulled his door shut and glanced down the hallway toward Deb. His goose was cooked if she watched with a pitiful look. *Would Stu promote another associate to partner?*

The thought twisted his gut into knots. He glanced down to inspect his shoes, then went down the hallway to where Stu had left his door partially open. Taking a deep breath, he tapped and stepped inside.

He recognized the man sitting in the conference chair. Gilbert Wallace, Michigan's Attorney General, caused Michael's gut another twist. He frantically searched his memory for any connection to the AG's office— anything he could have screwed up. Wallace read his mind.

"Relax, you're in no trouble. At least not yet," Wallace advised, with the slightest of smiles. "Sit down."

Stu motioned for Michael to take his chair. Wallace was clearly in charge of the meeting. "Excuse me," he leaned forward and extended his hand toward Michael. "Gilbert Wallace, Attorney General for the State of Michigan."

"Of course, sir. I recognized you immediately," Michael fawned, shaking the man's tanned hand. "What may I do for you?" Michael's wealthy upbringing gave him a particular aplomb in social events. He commonly encountered public figures. Business events, however, were completely different matters.

"You're familiar with recent election-denier events at the Capitol?"

"Who isn't?"

Wallace glanced at Taggert and continued. "Governor Page has ordered me to dump this case on lawyers better suited for its menial nature."

"Sir?" Michael was puzzled.

"Sorry. I guess you haven't heard about the lawsuit. Longhorn, Longfellow, Longest Yard, Long something or other—I don't remember the guy's name. That girl killed at the Capitol was this guy's only daughter, his pride and joy. You've seen one; you've seen them all. Man, I don't need to tell you."

"No, no, sir. You don't. Everyone wants to suck on the State's teat."

"Exactly. Here's the thing, Matthew."

"Michael."

"What's that?"

"Michael, sir. My name is Michael."

"Yeah, yeah, *Michael*. A lot on my mind today. So, Michael, uh, here's the thing. We live in a charged political atmosphere. There are troublemakers out there."

"I understand, sir."

"The governor won't make a big deal out of this even though he can score political points exploiting his predecessor's behavior. The media *loves* this kind of case. The governor is concerned about blowback from right-leaning and independent voters who switched their allegiance to restore normalcy and bipartisanship. God knows where this thing goes from here. The governor just assumed office. He's got enough on his plate without these annoying flies buzzing around his head."

Michael nodded and repeated, "I understand, sir."

"My office was set to handle the matter and sweep things under the rug. The young woman's family is just the old man, pretty near the grave by the looks of him. We intended to delay, deny, confuse, and refuse until the guy bought the farm." Michael encouraged Wallace to continue.

"The thing is—my office is under a lot of pressure. We can't add this to our calendar. I asked Stu to recommend someone, a young, good-looking go-getter eager to make his mark. He suggested you."

"Me, sir?"

"Yes, you, Martin. Your boss says you're a top litigator. You come from good stock. A well-connected family is good enough for me. I had some cases with your father back in the day. So, here I am, down from Lansing, to meet you in person, feel you out, and see if you might be a good fit. From my perch on high, you look mighty fine."

Michael turned from Wallace to Stuart, his sharp eyes seeking some giveaway. He *was* anxious to make his name, which was hard to do, coming from *his* family.

Michael's father, Stanley O'Hara, was a prominent lawyer, businessman, and politician. He served as Ambassador to Ireland during the Reagan years and was a huge fan of the former president and his politics.

At an early age, Michael was taught that the government could not do everything for everyone. The best thing the government could do was to clear the way for businesses and business owners to make their fortune. These businesses would, in turn, hire tax-paying workers, greasing the economic wheel for everyone. Michael worshipped his father and became a student of his business and legal philosophies.

The younger O'Hara was born and raised in the affluent suburb of Bloomfield Hills, received an exclusive private school education, and did his undergraduate work at the University of Michigan. His grades were excellent, and his postgraduate reputation was even better. He was accepted to the University's elite law school, where he graduated with honors. He was a sought-after graduate, but his father would only consider the top law firms in Detroit.

Stanley's political connections landed Michael a job at the Taggert firm. But Michael worked hard to *earn* the position. He was nobody's fool. His trial skills were superior, one reason his bosses recommended him for this assignment. Despite his recent failures in certain high-profile court appearances, Michael proved he could handle himself in a crisis. But what was at stake? *What if I fail? Am I willing to take this on? Willing to risk my partnership for this case?* He only took a moment to decide. *What choice do I have?*

"I'm honored, sir. My staff and I will immediately flyspeck every pleading and media report to date. Have someone in your office forward all relevant documents to me. I'm on this."

Stu spoke up. "The firm has already shifted your current clients elsewhere, Michael."

Michael's eyebrows rose. The decision was already made at the partner level. Michael either took Wallace up on his offer or had no cases or clients. This was the proverbial offer he couldn't refuse. The mob now dictated to the law rather than the other way around. He must win this case or kiss his partnership goodbye.

"That's very considerate of you, Stu. If there's nothing else, Mr. Attorney General, I'll get back to my office, call a staff meeting, and get things rolling."

"The sooner, the better. I'll send things over."

Michael glared at Stu. He knew this was payback for his recent courtroom failures. Taggert never praised Michael's success. In Michael's mind, he only kicked him when he was down. *Why does he always emphasize the negative? You're only as good as your last success.* Michael would embrace the assignment and demonstrate to Taggert that he was still a great litigator. Nothing would stand in his way.

Stu nodded, and Michael practically leaped from his chair and left the office, calling out orders as he strode down the hallway.

"Deb? I need anyone who's in my division here now. Put them all in the conference room and order in some deli. Cancel my dinner plans for tonight."

Michael hated to pass up a date with Vicki, but he had no choice. Taggert laid down the gauntlet. He had to prove himself *again*.

"Brock, get off your ass and find out about the firm that filed this lawsuit." He tossed the complaint on his junior associate's desk. "I want everything there is to know. What time do the firm members take a leak? Do the partners like oysters or clams? Who pisses who off? Are there women? Scandals? Illicit relationships? Who's screwing who? Got it?"

"Got it." Brock was the new boy on the block, a young associate, fresh out of the University of Detroit Law School. Michael walked in his shoes at one time. Brock would be a gopher until he paid his dues, or the higher-ups decided he earned something juicier.

With one mighty shout, Michael's voice was heard in every hallway, every office, and through every glass door.

"Anyone working in the office today, in the conference room, now!"

CHAPTER THREE

Andrea

"Won't you have a seat?" Andrea motioned to Longbow with unmanicured hands. After buying paint, office furniture, equipment, and supplies, she didn't have enough money for a manicure. Longbow looked down at the wooden dining table chair she'd stolen from her hand-me-down set and nodded, falling hard as though carrying a heavy burden. She could tell he was uncomfortable.

"Nice perfume you're wearing." He took her by surprise.

She stuttered, "Well . . . thank you." She'd spritzed more than usual, hoping it might cover the haunting smell.

"Now then," she began. "What's this about Governor Rinke and your daughter? Wh-what can I d-do for you? I mean . . . what *may* I do for you today?" *Damn nerves!*

Mr. Longbow looked at his hands in his lap as if to give her a moment to collect herself.

"Nice hat," she remarked, making conversation. There were loyal Detroit Tiger fans all over Michigan and beyond.

Lifting the hat off his head, he held it out for her to see and cleared his throat again. "My daughter gave me this hat on *her* birthday. Imagine that? A soul so sweet, she gives others presents on *her* birthday! My Marcy was like that. She claimed she didn't want to celebrate alone."

He leaned forward conspiratorially. "I knew what was going on, though."

Andrea, caught up in the moment's drama, leaned forward, her lips slightly agape. "What?"

"She didn't want to be alone—not on her birthday, not any other day. So, she'd give gifts to the people she wanted nearby. That way, they'd have to come to see her. Sort of an insurance policy that no one would forget her, you know?"

Andrea nodded, stone-faced. A calm demeanor was part of her job. Tough as nails—that was her motto. But she noticed that Longbow spoke of his daughter in the past tense.

"What happened to Marcy?" She cut to the chase.

He cleared his throat again, and not from smoking or pollution. He choked up. He dropped back against the chair, reached into his jacket pocket, and removed a crumpled handkerchief. She hadn't seen one of those in years. Her grandfather carried one back when he worked in his garden during the heat of August.

Mr. Longbow blew hard into the cloth, then folded it and returned it to its nest against his heart. Andrea could never understand how anyone could blow snot into a piece of cloth, place it back in his pocket, and constantly repeat the act.

"You heard about that nonsense stirred up by Rinke at the Capitol?" He trembled.

Andrea nodded again, prompting him to continue.

"Well, my Marcy doesn't send out gifts anymore. She'll have no more birthdays to celebrate. Rinke and his hooligans killed her."

Andrea gave him a couple of minutes to collect himself.

"Let me understand this," she finally replied. "Your daughter was the administrative assistant killed during the Capitol riots?"

He nodded. "Others died from circumstance, but those bastards *murdered* my Marcy."

Andrea pushed her chair back from the desk. Her heart hammered in her chest as she considered the ramifications of what success in such a case could do for her career. She swore she'd never take a case based on emotion alone. It was too easy to go off the rails and lose objectivity. It dulled the competitive senses. Yet, she heard herself say:

"I'll help you, Mr. Longbow."

He glanced up with eyes ringed in red. "I don't have much money."

"I'll handle the case on a contingency fee basis. You won't have to pay anything unless we win," she promised.

As reckless as it might seem to members of the public, her competition would promise the same arrangement. She sniffed at the air, deciding to get used to the smell—it wasn't going anywhere anytime soon. Hopefully, it would one day represent the sweet smell of success in the Longbow case.

***

"Sheila? It's Andi. How's everything?"

Sheila Corcoran was Andrea's law school roommate. They practically held hands on graduation day. It took both women a long time to get where they were, with multiple paybacks to be parceled out, especially between them.

"Fine, I guess. I had a cold last week, and my dog needs a vet."

"No, that's not what I meant. What are you doing these days? Do you have any big cases pending? Do you have free time?"

"Free time is all I have. Whoever said 'time is money' hasn't tried to build a law practice. Why? Have you got a bone to throw my way?"

Andrea spun around on the heel of her foot and slid into her chair, girding herself for the favor she was about to ask. She hesitated, knowing a thing or two about favors. They always had to be repaid in kind.

"Sheila, I'm up against the wall. I've got a high-profile case and no staff. I need help, and I was hoping you'd be willing."

"What's the pay?"

"Visibility? A part of the contingency fee if I'm successful? That's it. My client isn't well."

Sheila groaned from her side of the phone. "Come on, Andi. I've got rent to pay. The scuttlebutt suggests you're in the same boat. Are you working out of some haunted barn?"

"Not quite. Just a former residence with a sordid history."

"I have to eat."

"No problem. You can stay with me. I'll keep you fed. You won't be hungry for quite a while if things break our way."

"You mean if we win."

"No, I mean *when* we win."

"You sure know how to tighten the screws."

"I don't want to play dirty, but I remember a few exams where you might have fallen short. As I recall, I was the one who bailed *you* out."

"Oh, now you *are* playing dirty. Okay, how long will this take?"

"You have somewhere better to be?"

"I give up. I'll see you in the morning. Text me your new address."

Andrea rapidly tapped her cellphone keyboard. "Done. Wear your best clothes. You'll be on camera, and I don't mean just a snapshot. I'm throwing dice, and everything rests on this throw. See you tomorrow."

Andrea sat in her office the following morning, still sniffing the air. The main door opened with a jingle. "Welcome to Andrea Kramer and Associates," she called as she walked toward the lobby. Sheila Corcoran stood in the waiting room, looking around, sniffing the air.

"What's that smell?" Sheila wrinkled her nose, sniffing at the air.

Andrea walked up to her and gave her a quick hug. "What smell?"

"Seriously? You don't smell that? Come on, Andi!"

Andrea ignored her and pointed to a folding table across the room.

"That's your desk, specially selected for you," she giggled behind her hand. "No kidding. When this is over, we're even. You won't owe me anything else. And you might even score a large payday."

"If I don't, and I have a feeling I won't, you will owe me big time," Sheila threatened, tossing her briefcase and purse onto the table. She pushed down on the table to see how much weight it would bear.

"Note to self," Sheila joked. "Only sit in the chair. By the way, where's my chair?"

"Shit! I forgot. Be right back." Andi left the building and returned with a folding beach chair.

"Here you go. You can pretend you're on vacation while you work."

Sheila glared at the rickety old chair with the perforated webbing. She rolled her eyes and sighed.

"You sure know how to roll out the welcome mat or whatever that thing is."

"Okay, Sheila. You're here. There's no more time for small talk. We've got too much work to do. We'll catch up on life later while we cook dinner."

"We? I'm your guest. Guests don't cook."

"You're a worker bee, not a guest. If you want to eat, you'll help cook. I'll buy the food."

The women unconsciously lapsed into the good-natured sarcasm they once exchanged in college. It kept them warm during cold nights when both sat beneath a 40-watt bulb and crammed for exams. Adversity was a strong adhesive.

Andrea pointed to the chair. Sheila sat. Andi filled her in. She threw a nickel at Sheila, who caught it neatly, something she learned back in the day, selling lemonade on street corners.

"You're hired, co-counsel on the Longbow case. Everything we discuss from now on is strictly confidential. I won't lie. This case is far from easy. We will need everything we've learned in law school and in life to bring this one home. Want a baseball metaphor? We need a home run—singles are not acceptable. I've done a deep dive into the defense attorney, Michael O'Hara. He's a showboat who works for a big firm downtown. Arrogant and narcissistic, he makes *Rinke* look humble.

"I've been waiting for a case like this. I'm done with the dark side—I promised myself it would be payback time when I opened my office. I am in my office, Andrea Kramer & Associates, with no associates, only a building with a history and a strange smell. But it's mine, such as it is. It may not be much, but my name is on the door."

"So, you *do* admit there's an odor? I hope I survive this," Sheila groaned, sniffing at the air. "Let's have the details."

"Here, read." She tossed Sheila two small folders, all the paperwork accumulated to date.

"The young woman trampled at the Capitol?"

"The very same."

"I see now why you're so cloak and dagger. What's the current situation?"

"I filed the lawsuit and caught my first break. The case was assigned to Judge Rubin. He put the case on the rocket docket to move it along. I have a discovery order. We can expect a document dump," Andrea groaned. "Any day, a huge truck will pull up with hundreds of boxes of government files. We'll be knee-deep in paperwork.

"Enjoy reading and dealing with what we have so far. It shouldn't take long for you to get up to snuff. Okay?" Andrea started for the front door. "I'll see you later."

"Where the hell are you going?" Sheila demanded.

"I have a lunch meeting with this O'Hara guy. His office called and asked for a meeting, more like an off-the-record casual lunch. I'll bring you back something. You still like salami on rye?"

It wasn't typical for plaintiff and defense attorneys to enjoy a casual lunch at the beginning of what would soon become a hotly contested case. Andrea accepted the invitation to size up her opponent and, perhaps, pry out some inside information. She'd choke down a burger and guzzle a beer in the name of legal espionage. In the worst-case scenario, she'd get a free lunch.

Sheila gave her the stink eye. "It will do for a late lunch, but there had better be some corned beef, pastrami, or turkey for supper. Better yet, how about all three?"

"It's a deal. For now, look over the file, make a list, and devise a plan of attack, okay? We'll review things when I get back."

"I can handle that, so long as you satisfy my ravenous appetite, *boss*."

"Don't call me that," Andi called over her shoulder.

CHAPTER FOUR

THE MEETING

Andrea

Maggie Steiner was a bar and grill near the old shoe mill on the edge of town. At one time, the mill ran at total capacity, and Maggie dreamt of becoming rich. Ultimately, the war ended, crushing Maggie's dreams. These days, Maggie's granddaughter operated the dilapidated old railcar, which housed a couple of grills, a refrigerator, and an assortment of odds and ends tables and stools.

It was a place where locals hung out, and Michael O'Hara and Andrea Kramer met for lunch. Considering the Taggert firm's wealth and power, Andrea felt insulted but resolved to mask her feelings.

She knew it was Michael the minute he came into full view. She saw the fancy car pull up. A tall, handsome man with the bluest eyes she'd ever seen exited the vehicle with an arrogant smirk. She practiced planting *her* version of a smirk but doubted she could pull it off.

His blue eyes practically glowed from beneath a thick shock of black hair. He was neatly groomed, and the shoulder-length hair might have allowed him to play the title role in *Jesus Christ Superstar*. He looked out of place in Saline.

"Michael?" She called, waving. She stood, waiting for him to reach the table, holding out her hand to a man who might have adorned the cover of an illicit romance novel. The big city cover boy drew stares from every woman in the place.

Michael

"Andrea?" He took her hand, shook it gently, nodded, and gestured for her to sit. He wanted to be friendly but firm. He had a reputation and was determined to live up to it.

She's lovely. Michael attempted to hide his thoughts behind an orthodontic smile and an expensive custom-made suit. *Nice figure.* "It's a pleasure to meet you. I've heard a lot about you."

"Really? That's strange. I only opened my office last week."

"That's right. I forgot. I read about you. You're the attorney who recently moved into the haunted barn conversion in downtown Saline. Is Longbow your first client?"

Andrea's eyes narrowed. "So much for small talk, Mr. Congeniality, you invited me here. What's the deal? This may surprise you, but I'm a busy lady with a full schedule. You've come a long way to insult me. Consider me insulted, and I'll be on my way."

She stood. Michael stared her down, wondering if she'd leave. *This is a chess match on her home turf.* He was determined to stay competitive. There was too much at stake. He had a good case. If she decided to be rude, he'd be ruder. He'd play the long game and refuse to give an inch. This was a consistent pattern in his life, and his strategies usually worked.

"Of course, you will," he retorted, rolling his eyes. "Sit down, please. In consideration of your precious time, I'll be brief." Andrea sat.

"Because you're new to litigation at this level, I'll go easy on you. I'm sure you're second-guessing your decision to take on this complex matter. Frankly, it's quite a mess. Your complaint is a joke. You're about to get your ass kicked in court, considering the power and reputation of my firm and, of course, the client. But I am your proverbial white knight, here to let you off the hook."

Andrea leaned her head back and laughed out loud.

"You? You're nothing more than an errand boy, sent to frighten or pay me off. Was everyone else out of the office? More important things on their plates? On vacation in the tropics? I don't need to be let off the hook. I'll save *you* the embarrassment of a high-profile ass-kicking, Mr. Temporary Assistant Attorney General, sir.

"We can settle this right here now at this table, and you'll go home with your reputation intact. Or we can litigate this case. How will your country club partners react when a lowly sole practitioner, and a woman to boot, wins this so-called 'complex' litigation?"

Michael coughed. *How did she know?* He bent under the table, pulled a folder from his briefcase, slid it across the top, and tapped a finger on the jacket. His trial practice professor often demonstrated a leer he used for witness intimidation. Michael attempted his best impression.

"Check out the numbers in that folder. There's no admission of guilt involved. What do you think?"

"Not interested."

"You're not even going to look at it?"

"Oh, I've got a pretty good idea of what's in there. A lowball offer for a case of this magnitude will not interest my client."

"Your client has one foot on a banana peel and the other in the grave. You've got a lot to learn about negotiating, *lady*. Your client will be fortunate if he sees a dime before he dies. And that only happens if you accept the offer in that folder. There's even a cushion for a nice fee for your hard work. Maybe you can move out of that haunted barn."

Andrea again pushed her chair back and snapped to a stand.

"Watch this, *man*."

She turned and strolled out of the diner, deliberately teasing him, working her backside. Sheila greeted her as she slammed her way into the office.

"How did it go? Will there be enough for next month's rent?"

Andi was steaming. "What a cock, and I don't mean the bird."

CHAPTER FIVE

"Hey, Stan! How's everything?" One patron inquired. "Are we ever going to close that deal?"

"Entirely up to Art. He's dragging his feet. I'll light a fire under his ass and get things moving."

The man walked away as Michael O'Hara approached the booth and sat down. Father and son met for coffee at a popular diner in Bloomfield Hills. Stanley had breakfast at the place often enough to be called a 'regular.' Most of the staff and customers greeted him by name.

"Who's that, Dad? Anything I can do to help?" Michael wondered.

"Don Adler is a commercial real estate broker. Art Gardner is having a problem getting his buyer to the table. I was covering for him. It's an important deal—these things take time and finesse. Don has no patience. I'm holding the deal together with a Band-Aid. So, what did you want to talk to me about? Is everything okay at work? Taggert treating you well? If not, I know where all the bodies are buried."

"He's fine, Dad. I want to advance my career without you throwing your weight around. It's embarrassing. I want to be Michael O'Hara rather than Stanley O'Hara's son."

"I read you, son, loud and clear. Just trying to help."

A nice-looking, forty-something man walked by, wearing a high-fashioned tailored suit.

"Stanley O'Hara! Who are you shafting these days? You must love the new Democratic administration and legislative majority."

"Nice to see you, too, Zack. Did I ever rub Snyder in your face?"

"You didn't have to, Stan. He took care of that himself by poisoning the city of Flint."

"It's more complicated than that, and you know it."

"I know nothing of the sort. A blue-collar *Democratic* city falls on hard times—let's replace their pristine Detroit city water with polluted garbage from the Flint River. Who will notice? Isn't that about the size of it? After that fiasco, the best you can do is Rinke? Is there any limit to your party's ability to produce no talent, ethically challenged candidates?"

"Can we discuss politics another time? I'm having coffee with my son. He works for Stu Taggert's office. Michael? This annoying crusader is Zachary Blake, the self-proclaimed 'King of Justice.'"

"I've met your son," Zack nodded to Michael. "He's a fine lawyer—usually on the wrong side of things, but he's an excellent litigator. How's it going, Michael?"

"Great, Zack. Any recent eight-figure verdicts I should know about?"

"It's been quiet lately. I've got a couple of cases out of the Rinke insurrection. Nothing too serious. We'll see if they pan out. The way

Michigan corporate types misbehave, it won't be long before I get something big. For *now*, I'm just squeaking by.

"Your coffee is getting cold. I'll leave you to it. Good to see you guys." Zack walked away and sat in a corner booth on the other side of the diner.

"That's *his* booth. He comes in here every morning," Stanley advised Michael. "He's something else. He had a tough go, once upon a time, but he sure has the Midas touch these days, especially since that verdict against the Church."

"He *is* the real deal, every plaintiff lawyer's wet dream," Michael continued to eyeball Blake. "I've gone up against him a few times, but the cases settled early in the litigation."

"I'll bet you could handle him," Stanley boasted.

"I'm sure we'll wage war one of these days."

"What did you want to talk to me about?"

"I'm trying to read the tea leaves."

"About what?"

"Taggert dumped the Longbow litigation against the state of Michigan on my desk."

"Sorry, I'm not up to snuff. What's the Longbow litigation?"

"I'm sorry. I thought you knew. It's been in the news. Zack just alluded to the so-called Rinke insurrection. Arthur Longbow lost his daughter to the violence at the Capitol," Michael disclosed.

"Got it! I knew I recognized that name. What's the problem? Immunity protects the state, doesn't it?"

"Not if the plaintiff can prove gross negligence or some other exception to immunity, like the building exception," Michael advised.

"I'm sure you can handle it, son. What are you concerned about?"

"Attorney General Wallace is a close friend. Why isn't Taggert handling this case?"

"He's the boss. He can choose what and what not to handle. That's his prerogative," Stanley reasoned.

"I guess, but I feel like I'm being set up. If the case is a loser, Taggert blames me for the loss and comes out smelling like a rose with the AG."

"That's pretty cynical, don't you think, son?"

"I've been the firm's best litigator, Dad. Lately, I've had a few bumps and bruises. This is either a set-up or a comeuppance of sorts."

"You've answered your question, Michael. You're the firm's best litigator. Who else would they give this case to if not their best litigator?" Stan rationalized.

"I guess you're right, but I have a bad feeling about it."

"Who's on the other side?"

"A relative newcomer named Andrea Kramer. She's been out of law school for only a few years. She recently hung her shingle—practices out of some converted, haunted barn and silo in Saline. Some family was murdered there. Andrea is not only smart; she's a stunner." Michael looked starry-eyed.

"Interesting story about the building *and* the lawyer. Keep it in your pants, son," Stanley warned. "Do not, under any circumstance, mix business with pleasure. Think with your head, not with your dick. And don't underestimate this woman."

"I'm not stupid, Dad. This is the biggest case of my career. I bring up her looks only because she will play well before a jury. She'll have a fabulous courtroom presence."

"And you're a great-looking young man, Michael. Juries love you, especially the females. Stack the jury with ladies, son!"

"Easier said than done. You don't think I'm being set up to fail?"

"As I said, I think they gave their biggest case to their best litigator. What would you have them do? Stop worrying about Taggert, the AG, and this Kramer woman. Just do what you've been trained to do. Litigate the case and kick the lady's ass."

"I feel better already. Thanks, Dad. Want to order?"

CHAPTER SIX

Michael

"I have things under control," Michael assured Stuart Taggert. After breakfast with his father, Michael returned to the office to review case developments with the senior partner. Taggert fidgeted, loosened his tie, and checked his fingernails.

"I'm not so sure," Stu countered. "I had the investigator check out this Kramer woman. She's the real deal—graduated summa cum laude from U of M, has yet to blossom, but is an untapped talent awaiting the right opportunity. Longbow might be that opportunity. Don't underestimate her. And, if that isn't enough, she's *very* easy on the eyes. The jury will love her." Taggert pulled Andrea's headshot out of a thin file.

"I'm the first to acknowledge her physical attributes, Stu. I've seen her in person. We had lunch.

"I talked with my dad about the case, her inexperience, and how she might appeal to a jury, especially a *male* jury. But I can keep men off the jury, and she will get her ass handed to her in court. Beautiful and smart or not, she's a newbie, arrogant, too sure of herself, and most of all, I made things *personal.* She now hates my guts.

"She'll come out of her corner fighting. I'll give her the old rope-a-dope or Ali shuffle, the dodge and weave, and let her punch herself out." Michael pushed past Stu gracefully. "Join me for a shot?" An afternoon drink was a semi-ritual.

"Nope. I need a clear head—too much going on. I'm quite concerned about this case. So are the other partners. I'm getting a lot of pressure, and not just within the office. This type of case can make or break a law firm. The AG's office is on my ass."

Michael nodded. Stu's comment made him wonder again if he was being scapegoated. He brushed away the negative thoughts and motioned for Stu to sit while he opened the right-hand bottom drawer of his desk. He pulled out a bottle of bourbon and a shot glass. His hand trembled slightly as he poured. Before saying another word, he drained the glass, put everything back into the drawer, and snapped it shut with his foot. It was routine for Michael; he'd done it many times before. He paused, studying his boss.

"I get it, Stu. She wants to showboat, demonstrate she belongs, and secure a seat at the table with the big boys. You and I know that if anybody can play that game, it's me."

Stu crossed his legs. He studied a bird that chanced to land on the narrow sill outside Michael's window. It wasn't often that birds came that close and that high, except for pigeons. Pigeons seemed to have no limits.

"I'll leave you to it, Michael. The staff and the resources are yours. The sky's the limit. Either settle this quietly or win at all costs."

"Understood, boss. I'll spend tonight rounding out my plan. Tomorrow morning, I'll call a meeting and begin delegating responsibilities. Kramer was pretty much what I expected, perhaps a tad better looking. It'll give me something to stave off the boredom."

"You called her arrogant, but that seems to go double for you. Don't get too cocky, Michael."

"But that *is* the idea, isn't it?"

"Wait a minute. Are you going after the girl?"

"Not exactly. I want to throw her off her game. I'll do whatever needs to be done."

"Hold the phone, Michael. I'm not sure I'm on board with your so-called strategy. This case is too important."

"Relax," Michael advised. "I don't want to reveal too much. Stay tuned as the strategy plays out."

"It's probably not necessary to tell you this, but your future with this firm depends on the outcome of this case. You get that, right?" Stu stood to leave.

Michael's head snapped up. His eyes met Stu's. He probed his expression, hoping the man was kidding. Stu's deadpan eyes said otherwise. Michael was on probation with more than a partnership on the line. His first instincts were correct. He *was* the scapegoat. His *career* was at stake.

Stu exited the office. Michael dropped into his chair and swiveled to gaze over the skyline. He was afraid of heights, an insecurity he rarely acknowledged—*never show the enemy your weakness.* Looking out over the skyline was his way of confronting hidden fears. He did it often, a rehearsal for the courtroom, a nasty opponent or judge, his version of behavior modification. Like playing chicken as a teenager, drag racing down a straight stretch of country road.

Sometimes, he wished life was simpler—he longed for those country roads, his souped-up hot rod, and the wind blowing through his long, dark hair. When he was a kid, his parents spoiled him, doted on him, and gave him everything a kid could want. He was the envy of all his friends. The younger Michael didn't have to worry about making partner or getting involved in career-threatening litigation. He suddenly felt light-headed and had difficulty identifying buildings, parks, and streets outside his window.

He swiveled around, picked up a pen, and grabbed company letterhead from a wire basket on his immaculate desk. He doodled, his way of focusing on the matter at hand. He always neatly folded his finished doodle sheets, placed them into his breast pocket, and took them home to discard. He was meticulous about cleaning up after his weaknesses, just as he was about the people he invited into his life.

For a relative rookie, Andrea Kramer showed more guts and grit than he expected. He tried to remember what it felt like when he was assigned his first big case. He sensed that Andrea lacked the necessary resources for a case like Longbow—he reviewed the investigator's file, cover to cover. She had limited experience and was young and alone. She'd have to scramble. He'd take advantage of these shortcomings. Maybe he'd have to be a prick, *but anything for the win.*

Michael tapped his fingers noisily on the desk surface. "Damn!" He slapped the top of his desk, rose, and walked to the coffee room. He grabbed a mug reserved for attorneys and poured himself a cup of Jamaican brew from the decanter.

He once lobbied for a Keurig machine, but the partners were a frugal trio and considered it a newfangled fad device. However, they did stock a brand of coffee beans, freshly ground before each brewing.

Michael returned to his office, closed the door, and pulled the drapes. Anyone who knew him could see he was bothered. He woke his computer and typed 'Andrea Kramer, Saline, Michigan lawyer' into the search bar.

Like Michael, she graduated from Michigan with honors. She came from a small, humble family in a small town. Her parents were both teachers. They were also Democratic rabble-rousers back in the day. Right-wingers might have called them *radicals.* Andrea held leadership positions throughout high school, college, and law school. Academic and employment histories were glowingly positive. She never married.

Michael wondered whether this was an important tidbit of information. Maybe she was too busy with school, making a career for herself. *What's with this woman? She's pursuing a case with political consequences. She might hurt more than her career. It's unsafe. For her or me?* Michael O'Hara felt himself sinking into quicksand.

CHAPTER SEVEN

Andrea

Andrea stopped by the coffee shop on her way to the office to pick up her usual thermos of coffee and some chocolate doughnuts. She had a few extra minutes, so she slid neatly into a booth, plopped her handbag on the table, and promptly knocked the saltshaker onto the floor. She cringed as she peered below the table surface. Salt had sprayed a considerable arc—which, in her opinion, presented a potential liability hazard. Mary Beth wandered over to the table and sized up the mess.

"Oh, honey, don't worry about that. These things happen all the time. Pull your legs back—I'll grab my broom, and we'll have this cleaned up in no time."

"I'm so sorry to cause you extra trouble. If you get me the broom, I'll gladly sweep it up."

"No, honey, you're the customer. Besides, you've got enough problems of your own." Mary Beth's eyes diverted to the floor.

"What do you mean?"

"I mean—" Mary Beth hesitated and looked around to see who else was sitting nearby. "What do I mean? Someone's been asking around about you. No secret who's behind it."

"Me? How do you know?"

"Honey, you don't do what I do this long and not get a feel for what's happening around town. Lots of people have your back, whether you know it or not. They rooted for you all through college and law school. I've never heard a bad word said about you."

Andrea glowed with the warm feeling of her supportive hometown. Was O'Hara snooping about? She imagined he left quite a trail of broken hearts and angry vengeance. *It probably gives him pleasure. He wears it like a badge of honor.*

"I appreciate that, Mary Beth. But what people are asking about me, and what are they asking? Do you have any more specifics?"

"Do I need any?" Mary Beth grabbed a broom from the corner and bent forward, slowly guiding the slippery salt particles toward the open mouth of a dustpan. "Don't worry, no one will tell that lawyer anything unless, of course, it's good. We take care of our own."

"Geez, that might make him suspicious. No one is perfect."

"As far as we're concerned, you are. And we'll smell a rat no matter who he sends out to collect intel. Nobody's getting anything out of us."

Andrea nodded. Mary Beth walked away to tend to other customers. She returned briefly to deposit coffee and donuts, giving Andrea an exaggerated wink. Andrea nodded back but was seething inside.

How dare he come to my town asking questions? Reconnaissance on Andrea's client or his daughter was one thing. Any thorough attorney would've done the same. Check out her legal pedigree? Fair game, if limited to her education, specialty, licensing, and practice.

But digging into her personal life was off-limits. Dirty pool. *Is this ethical? If he wants to play by those rules, I'll give that prick a run for his money. Two can play that game.*

Twenty minutes later, she burst through her office door, causing Sheila to look up in alarm. "What on earth?"

Andrea slammed her purse onto the desk, knocking her little cactus plant onto the floor. She grimaced—*another clean-up.*

"Want me to get that for you?"

"No! I did it. I'll clean it up."

"Why don't you give yourself a few minutes? You're annoyed about something. The plant is prickly—so are you. You're liable to poke yourself, which will only cause further aggravation. What's going on?" Sheila was concerned.

"The nerve of that man!"

"Whoa, calm down. Who put a bee in your bonnet?"

"O'Hara is having me investigated. Can you believe that?"

"Of course, I can. I'd do the same thing. He can't do some hatchet job character assassination on your client. The man is old and weak. A jury won't appreciate that. On the other hand, if he poisons the prospective jury pool with rumors about the attorney . . . You are fair game, Andi," Sheila argued.

"You took this case. You've got to live with the scrutiny that comes with high-profile litigation. Man up, woman! He's looking for dirt— something you've hidden, hoping it would never resurface. Makes perfect sense to me. As I indicated, I'd do the same thing. *You* should investigate *him*," Sheila suggested.

"I agree, but I'm surprised *you* feel that way."

"Grow up. I repeat—this is high-stakes litigation. The winner takes all. It is not a gentleman's game or for the faint of heart. If you aren't up to it, step aside. Mr. Longbow can find someone willing to fight dirty to win his case. Get down in the mud and fight back, bee-otch! When O'Hara goes low, you go lower," Sheila snarled.

"I don't believe I'm hearing this from you. In law school, everything had to be by the book."

"Law school was *theory*, background for a possible career. After three years of hard labor, what do you have? You can go to work for a small firm and be a worker bee. You can draft wills and estates, review contracts, or help criminals evade justice. You can teach or work for the government. Law school does not teach the cutthroat, dog-eat-dog *business* of litigation. The strong survive—the weak are gobbled up. Politics get in the way. We've seen that play out on cable news." Sheila swiveled in an ancient office chair, turning her back on Andrea.

"I know you think I'm a pansy; you always have. You have no idea what makes me tick. You think I'm here because you need help. Get over yourself. I'm here to bask in the limelight and have my piece of the rags-to-riches American dream. This is the quickest way to get where I want to go. I've struggled, just like you. Clients are not exactly breaking down my door."

"What's your endgame?" Andrea asked.

"I'm going to be governor someday. I've already decided," Sheila sighed.

"Holy shit, Wonder Woman! Why stop there? Isn't the country ready for a female president?" Andrea chuckled.

"Now you're getting the idea. Until now, I've been biding my time, handling two-bit cases. I'm better than that! This is my big chance, a case about dirty politics ending in tragedy. I want to dip my toes in the water and pop my head above the crowd. I want the powers that be to remember my name and where they heard it. 'That's the woman who helped Andrea Kramer kill it on that Longbow case against the state.'"

"Wow. You are full of surprises. I had no idea you had these kinds of aspirations."

"You need to become a better judge of character. Start with that narcissistic defense lawyer, O'Hara. Besides, he's easy on the eyes. Haven't you noticed?"

"Maybe he can bat his baby blues at female jurors and get what he wants, but his charm won't work on me."

"So, you *did* notice the color of his eyes?"

***

"Hey girl, how's it going?"

"G . . . great . . . Becky? Is that you? How long has it been?"

A soft laugh drifted over the line. "It *has* been a while. You almost forgot about your old best friend. Too busy, I suppose."

"It's so great to hear your voice! Where are you? Can we get together?"

"Yes. Do you have time for lunch? I know it's last minute, but I want to run something by you."

"Of course, I have time for my best friend from high school. I've missed you! How many nights did we help each other through our deepest insecurities, boy trouble, teachers, dresses for the homecoming dance or the prom? God, girl, it seems so long ago." Yet here she was on the other side of the phone. Andrea didn't hesitate.

"Name the place."

"The usual? Twelve-thirty?"

"I'll be there."

The Meltdown hadn't changed much since Andrea went away to college and law school. She pulled into the parking lot. Suddenly, ten years dropped away. Pulling open the door, the familiar aroma of deep-fried, beer-battered onion rings and outdoor chargrilled burgers permeated the dining room.

She spotted Becky in their favorite booth from back in the day. Toward the rear of the restaurant, near the kitchen door, it was noisy enough to cover their gossip. Besides, they always got excellent service. Becky had a crush on the son of the restaurant owner. The son used to help his dad after school and on weekends, which Becky, strangely, found romantic.

Andrea teased her about the boy, suggesting his hands were always greasy. Becky ignored her. She was like that—self-determined, she never took anything or anyone too seriously. Andrea heard through the grapevine that Becky was engaged to the hamburger boy.

Becky approached her—arms open for a big reunion. "Oh, my God, Andrea, it's so good to see you again!" Becky effused, with tears in her eyes. "You look terrific! I've missed you. I have followed all your accomplishments over the years. I'm so proud of you."

"I've missed you, too. You look great! I can't wait to catch up. Let's sit down and get out of the way," she suggested, nodding toward the open booth. Just as they sat down, a man approached them and addressed Andrea.

"How are you doing, Andi?"

"Bran? Is that you?"

"It's me, in the flesh." He pulled on his protruding stomach flab. "Get it? In the flesh?" He laughed.

Andrea's mouth dropped open as she eyed her friend. "Are you two married?"

Becky shook her head. "No, we're not married, not yet. We're, shall we say, exploring options." She shot Bran a seductive smile.

"I'm ready for all the details, Becky. Good to see you again, Bran."

"The feeling is mutual. The usual?"

"You remember?" Andrea asked.

"I never forget a food order," Bran assured.

Andrea looked at Becky and back to Bran. She grinned and nodded. "Bring it on, Bran, the hamburger man!"

As Bran walked off, the two old friends dissolved into conversation and reminiscences about the old days.

"Remember the time we met at the community center dance?" Becky recalled. "I was volunteering. Brandon was there. He came up to me after the dance and asked for my number. We've been together ever since."

Andrea remembered. "I also remember how we hung out here at the restaurant so you could flirt with him."

"Sure did," Becky laughed at the memory. "I'm so glad I did. He's the love of my life."

They continued to chat and catch up on old times, eating, drinking, talking, laughing, and reminiscing until it was time for Andrea to leave.

Andrea gathered her things. Becky ventured, "There's this new lawyer in town. He's been asking around, checking you out. I thought you ought to know."

"That's interesting. Tell me more," Andrea prompted.

Becky nodded. "He's from Detroit. Here on business."

Michael! "What did you tell him?"

Becky laughed. "I told him you were single and would be *very* interested in someone tall, well-built, and handsome. He's easy on the eyes. I tried to spice things up . . . you know . . . help a friend."

Andrea shook her head. "You're terrible! I can't believe you did that. I don't need to be fixed up."

Becky grinned. "Perhaps, but he seemed interested. The question is, why aren't you?"

Andrea leaned over the table. "I don't mix business with pleasure. The guy you're talking about is my opposing counsel on a big case. That's a no-no in legal circles, regardless of how good-looking he is."

Becky continued. "But he's drop-dead gorgeous!" Her face softened. "I'm sorry, Andi. I didn't consider the whole business-pleasure thing. I didn't mean to cause trouble."

Andrea sighed. "You didn't cause trouble. I'm a big girl. Besides, it's more his fault than yours. I'm not surprised he wandered into this place asking questions. Thanks for trying to play matchmaker."

Becky grinned sheepishly. "Any time. How shall I put him off the scent?"

"I'm not entirely sure yet. I'm still formulating my master plan," Andrea snarled.

"Do you like him? Even a little? He's quite the looker."

Andrea scrunched her lips to one side. "He *is* nice looking. I can't say I know him very well. Looks may be deceiving. He's arrogant. Why would a woman be interested in a guy who may love himself more than her? Besides, we *are* on opposite sides of a case. He may just be *pretending* to be interested. I'm more focused on the case than the guy. Understood?"

"Absolutely."

Andrea mulled over the conversation as she drove back to her office. She had never been the subject of an investigation. She understood the concept of opposition research, but she wasn't comfortable with the idea. *Does he think I'm an easy target? If so, he's messing with the wrong woman!*

She decided to give him a taste of his own medicine—confuse him so badly he'd have no idea what hit him. She would use his vanity against him. *Serves him right for being so presumptuous.* She grinned to herself, already plotting the demise of Michael O'Hara.

CHAPTER EIGHT

Andrea

Andrea looked up to see Mr. Longbow standing in her doorway. His face was sallow, his posture hunched as he leaned against the doorframe.

"Sorry to drop in without an appointment, Ms. Kramer, but I just got released from the hospital. Stopped here on my way home."

"Hospital, Mr. Longbow?" Andrea came around her desk, quickly stepping in to take his arm and lead him to a chair. "Please, have a seat."

He ignored her invitation and stood in front of her. "I'm sorry to say I have some bad news."

"What is it?" Her voice was tight, her hands clenched into fists.

"I've had a heart attack."

Andrea's stomach dropped. This was not what she wanted to hear. "I'm so sorry," she replied, meaning it. "Is there anything I can do?"

"You know the law like the back of your hand, right?" He looked at her with hopeful eyes.

"I'm not sure about that," she confessed, "but I know it as well or better than the next lawyer. What I don't know, I can research. What's on your mind?" *Where's he going with this?*

"I want to add *my* claim to the lawsuit—sue the state for causing me stress. They're responsible for my heart attack." His voice was weak but determined. "They're trying to *kill* me, just like my daughter."

Andrea frowned. "That's an entirely different matter, Mr. Longbow, but I will research and investigate such a claim. You have my word."

"No, on second thought," he immediately reconsidered, falling into the chair in front of Andrea's desk. "Let's drop the whole thing. This is all too much for me."

"Are you sure?" Andrea groaned. "Most of the work falls on my shoulders. I'm willing to take them on. You won't have to do much."

"Is it worth it? A lawsuit won't bring my daughter back," he lamented with a tired sigh. "What's done is done."

Andrea wanted to accept his decision but was determined to pursue the case. She presumed Marcy wouldn't have given up without a fight.

"They are guilty of your daughter's wrongful death, Mr. Longbow. They had a duty to protect her."

"I know," he shook his head from side to side. "But like I said, what's done is done."

"There's too much at stake here, sir. We've gone this far, filed the lawsuit, and spent a lot of energy and money. We can't let this go unpunished. What about the next person's daughter? I am asking for your permission to continue. As I told you earlier, I'll continue to handle everything on a contingency and advance all costs. It won't cost you a dime."

"You're sure? You can afford that?"

"I believe in justice, Mr. Longbow," she continued. "And I believe in your case. I will do everything possible to get you the compensation you deserve. Besides, I *promised* to handle this on a contingency. A promise is a promise."

He nodded, overcome with emotion. "Alright, thank you," he whispered. "Thank you so much."

She nodded. "I'll be in touch, sir. You take care of yourself. Leave the case to me."

Her heart ached for him as she watched him leave. *I must get this poor man justice.*

Michael

"What did you find out?" Michael asked the private investigator he hired to check out Andrea.

"She's a model citizen, I'm afraid. I couldn't find any dirt on her at all. You believe she has a hidden past?" The investigator scanned his notes.

He paused the review and peered at Michael over the top of his glasses. "She's squeaky clean. Are you sure there's something there?"

"No, but no one is perfect. There must be *something*." Michael tried to *will* the existence of a scandal.

"I'll have to figure out some other angle or line of inquiry. Nothing came out in my typical background check."

Michael leaned back in his chair. He knew to avoid burning bridges with people who could dig up dirt.

"Thanks for trying, Jimbo. Maybe I'll go down there and do a little amateur sleuthing."

"Knock yourself out. If you want my opinion, you're wasting your time."

After the investigator left, Michael packed a few things. He was confident he would find something on Andrea to assist him in the lawsuit. Everyone had at least one skeleton in their closet. He was determined to find Andrea Kramer's.

***

Michael had hoped to find *something* to leverage, some dirt, *somewhere*. Her old high school chum had loose lips but knew nothing suggestive or inappropriate. He made a few notes and picked up the phone to signal his secretary.

"Deb, I need you to make some hotel or motel arrangements. I'm going down to Saline for a few days. Is there a decent hotel nearby?"

"I'll find someplace suitable," Deb promised.

"Thanks," Michael replied, disconnecting. He and Deb had a long-term understanding. While she detested his tactics, she needed the job and knew who the boss was.

On the other side, Michael knew how difficult it was to find a terrific secretary, especially one who tolerated him. The two developed and treated one another with professional respect, even if they could not resolve all differences.

Michael leaned back in his chair, closed his eyes, and smiled. *Playing detective for a change might be fun.* And if it meant he could dig up some dirt on Andrea, perhaps annoy the shit out of her, it was worth it. Ultimately, he would use anything he found in court. Nothing and no one would stop him from winning this lawsuit. Certainly *not* Andrea Kramer.

Michael rented a car for his trip. His Jag was too flashy—it would stand out in Saline. *Better to tone it down a bit.* Deb booked him into a sleepy little roadside motel, left over from the 1950s when Saline was a thoroughfare of travel.

"It's the best I could find," she apologized.

Michael drove to Saline without consequence and checked into the little motel. A scent of decay and aging pine logs, cosmetically altered by plug-in room air fresheners, struck him head-on. However, the bedcovers were neat, and the pillowcases were ironed by hand. He could tell.

A man who never does laundry can tell what comes from a professional laundry. He pulled back the coverlet and threw it on the room's second double bed. He opened his suitcase and removed a sleeping bag he had compressed into a plastic storage bag. He tossed it on the bed. There was no point in opening it before he needed to. It would keep him safe—at least as safe as necessary.

Michael picked up a glass from a tray by the television. Holding it up to the light, he checked for fingerprints. To his surprise, it was spotless. He walked to the bathroom sink, washed the glass, pulled bottled water from his bag, and poured some into the glass. Michael walked outside, found an old but functional ice machine, and added a few ice cubes. He returned to the room, sat on the bed, and surveyed his surroundings. *I'll tolerate the place long enough to get what I came for.*

Jimbo gave him Andrea's office address, those of her friends, and the places she frequented. Michael took a reconnaissance drive and checked out all the addresses, seeking a flavor of the beautiful and mysterious Andrea Kramer. Nothing stood out as unusual or unsavory. *A model citizen,* as the investigator reported. He was disappointed. *Can anyone be this clean?*

Michael returned to the motel, changed into jeans and a flannel plaid shirt, and drove to the bar Jimbo mentioned. He chose a corner seat, passed on the hard stuff, and ordered a beer. He nursed it, waiting. He was early and had a long wait. At seven-thirty that evening, Andrea walked into *The Meltdown.* He watched as she ordered a glass of wine, found an empty table for two, opened a notebook she pulled from her purse, and began making notes.

"Good evening."

Andrea appeared annoyed with the initial interruption. When she looked up and saw Michael, she huffed and groaned.

"Hello." Andrea's eyes bobbed back and forth, tracking her notes. "What are you doing here?"

"I get it. I'm the enemy. The notes have something to do with the case. I'm the last person you want looking over your shoulder while you're working."

She slapped the notebook shut and glared up at him, exasperated. "Is there something I can do for you? I'm rather busy."

He pointed to the chair opposite her. "May I sit?"

Andrea stood to leave. After doing an abrupt one-eighty, she smiled and pointed to the chair.

"Suit yourself. New in town? *Of course,* you are. Lost? Why else would you lower yourself and venture into small-town America?"

"Cute, Kramer. Very cute. What makes you think I'm lost? Perhaps I've found exactly what I was looking for."

The double entendre was unavoidable. No one was more surprised than Michael. He flushed slightly, embarrassed, a rare emotion. Andrea maintained a smug, self-righteous look on her face. Michael knew that Andrea knew why he was there. She was no slouch.

"So, what can I do for you?" She demanded.

At that moment, a rather stout young woman approached the booth. Her large boobs stretched out her thin T-shirt, emphasizing the words written across her chest, "Give it to me one more time."

"Andi!" She crowed. "Wow, I haven't seen you in ages. I thought you got married."

"Karen? It is Karen, right? Been a long time," Andrea grimaced.

"Of course, it's Karen! Don't mess with my head, silly."

Oblivious to Andrea's displeasure at the interruption, Karen reached behind her and produced a cute little redhead about three years of age.

"This is Thomas. We call him Beaver, like the old TV show from the 60s. He's not the sharpest knife in the drawer, but he's still young. Keeps me busy. So, *are* you married?" She stopped to admire Michael. "Is this stud muffin your husband?"

"In his dreams. No, I'm not married. I went to college and law school. I just opened my own law office."

"Right . . . now that you mention it, I remember hearing something about that. The old, haunted place. Wow, Andi Kramer, attorney at law."

"Does that surprise you?" Andrea grumbled.

"No, not at all. You always were the best at everything you did. You were the only girl on the debate team. I remember I dated a boy on that team. Didn't last long because, let's face it, like Beaver here, I'm not all that bright either. That guy was upper tier, although he did enjoy *my* upper tier . . ." She cupped her massive breasts. Andrea looked away.

"After sampling the merchandise, he lost interest in me. I can't say I blame him—we weren't a match. I remember going up against a team from Sterling Heights. I tagged along for moral support.

"My guy got asked some complicated questions and got flustered. I never saw him flustered like that. He turned to you, pleading for you to bail his ass out. You stepped in, took over the debate, and impressed everyone. All the guys were in awe—they weren't used to being bested by a girl."

"I'm still surprising the guys," Andrea smirked at Michael. "Besting them, too. It's great to see you again, Karen. Nice chatting with you about the old days. Would you excuse us, please? This gentleman drove some distance to talk to me."

"Sure, sure, no problem. Sorry. Good to see you, too. Hope to see you around."

Karen hustled Beaver toward the door, waving over her shoulder. Andrea watched as she climbed into an aging Jeep Cherokee. When she started the vehicle, the tailpipe emitted a gray cloud of smoke.

"Old school chum?" Michael observed.

"You heard her. We went to high school together. We were once close. She was always a friendly person—we had different life goals. Still, she's someone I would consider a friend. Surprised? Not cultured enough for you?"

"I wonder if your talents might be more appreciated in a big city environment. You could help more people, right?"

Andrea tapped the table before she replied. Her response was terse. "No, these are my people. They need me more than any of those big spenders in the city. I can make a difference here. Less politics. Besides, I thought you liked small-town law."

"I've never practiced small-town law."

"Give it a try sometime. So, are you here to badmouth my town, or do you have another reason to visit? A little intel, perhaps?"

"You've got me. Surprised?"

Andrea chose her words carefully. "No, not at all. You have a reputation, you know, very thorough. It's how you set traps for the opposition." A smile crossed his face and crept into his eyes.

"Why, thank you."

"So . . . I'll ask again. What are you doing here?" She waved her arm out to her fellow diners in the restaurant. "Isn't this a little out of your comfort zone?"

The door opened, and feet stomped on the wood floor. Andrea swiveled and saw Homer Dunlap. His shoes shed something that could only have come from the fields. The rancid smell quickly permeated the small restaurant and choked everyone up. After a short break, everyone returned to their soups and sandwiches.

Michael pulled a starched white handkerchief from his inner pocket and dabbed at his nose. He pushed away the menu that lay before him.

"Like I told you, O'Hara. My people," Andrea grinned.

"Maybe I'll have an early dinner and hit the hay. This country air is quite . . . intoxicating. I may not be able to keep my eyes open."

"Lost your appetite?" She inquired. "The sights and smells of Saline are not to your liking?" She pinched the bridge of her nose.

Michael watched her eyes dance, her nose crunch, and her bottom lip quiver. She was utterly kissable.

"Well, I wouldn't be quite that blunt."

"It's okay. People around here might be offended by that cologne that you spritzed on this morning. While it might seem natural to you, there isn't a cow that would come within ten yards of anyone who smells like that."

"Should I feel regret or gratitude?"

"To each his own," she retorted. "If you're not going to ask me whatever nosy questions you planned to ask when you moseyed over here, how about you get along with your day, and I'll return to mine? I've got work to do." She tried to dismiss him.

Suddenly, Homer Dunlop, the 'shit-shoes guy,' stood at the booth. "If it ain't Andi Kramer."

"Hello there, Homer. Didn't I see you at church on Sunday? That you who snuck out the back door just as your wife got up to sing with the choir?"

"You ain't going tell her, are you? She thinks I went to the restroom."

Andrea symbolically zipped her mouth closed with a hand gesture. "Not a word from me, Homer. Listen, man, this guy is leaving." She pointed to Michael on the opposite side of the booth. "Won't you join me? I'd love to catch up." She invited him to take the seat Michael still occupied.

"Don't mind if I do." Homer started to push Michael into the inside position in the booth. Michael quickly scooted out, stood, and signaled for Homer to take his place. As he turned to leave, he paused, about to say something. He quickly thought better of it. Getting into it with Andrea in a place where she knew everyone was not wise.

"No more Mister Nice-Guy, Kramer. See you at the motion for summary disposition," he muttered, looking back to her as he walked out the door. Andrea giggled when Michael O'Hara and his fancy shoes stepped into whatever Homer Dunlop shed onto the floor.

CHAPTER NINE

Andrea

Andrea arrived at the office early the following morning, having slept in fits and spurts the night before. Her blankets ended up on the floor next to the bed. A trail of clothing led to the hamper in the bathroom. Habitually tidy, she turned and cursed the mess, promising to address it tomorrow.

She turned on the coffeepot and searched for a can of coffee. She found the empty can in the garbage. "Damn!"

If there was ever a time when she needed a good cup of coffee, this was it. She thought about going to the diner or coffee shop but knew she couldn't resist the doughnuts. Sugar made her antsy and caused added pounds. She needed to be in fighting shape for the trial.

Resigned to a morning without caffeine, she flicked off the coffeepot, returned to her desk, unlocked an old file cabinet, and removed the Longbow file. The case was moving along on the docket. A discovery order had been entered. The case dominated her time and brought in *zero* revenue.

Could she squeeze in something less challenging, a misdemeanor assignment, perhaps a will, anything that might generate some income?

Sheila would help. Money was now an issue. The rent was due, and her savings account was close to depleted. She drifted off in her chair but was startled awake by a deep voice.

"I hear you're meeting with the enemy."

"What? Oh, I'm sorry. I didn't hear you come in, Mr. Longbow. Please, have a seat." She pointed to the chair opposite her desk.

"No, I don't think so. I'm not sure that I can trust you."

"Why would you think that? I'm the one taking all the financial risk. Hopefully, you appreciate what that means," she tried to explain.

"If we lose the case, this is all for nothing. My practice dies here and now, you're my first and last client, and I will have to find a job somewhere. Can't you see that my incentive to win is strong? Where's this coming from?" Andrea demanded.

He sauntered over to the chair, walking with greater difficulty than ever before. Leaning his hand on the chairback, he eased himself down until seated. Pain brought a grimace to his face.

"Why are people seeing you around town with this guy? Is that kosher? Shouldn't you be working for Marcy? Do you care about the memory of my daughter?

"I don't even have an heir to leave money to if I win the case. With appeals, this could drag on forever. Isn't that their strategy? Wait me out? See if I die before the case is finished? Besides, they've got deep pockets. You don't," Longbow sighed.

Andrea nodded, closing her eyes to concentrate.

"Everything you just said is true."

"So? What's the deal?"

"Taking on this case is probably the dumbest thing I've ever done unless you count the time I parked with Bobby Robbins."

Longbow didn't crack a smile. Nothing was funny to this man who lost so much.

"I do this work for the *community,* Mr. Longbow. Marcy isn't the only reason. I help people in pain or who have suffered a loss. Maybe they live in utter misery because someone messed up their lives. If I'm successful with your case, I can take important cases for clients in similar situations and help *them* in the future. Don't you see?" Andrea pleaded.

"Everything is a matter of perspective. I wanted to avenge my daughter. I couldn't let that crazy ex-governor and his cronies get away with murder. Somewhere along the way, though, I wondered why I started this. We can't win. In my heart, I knew that from the beginning.

"I'm old enough to know you can't go against the political machine without getting chewed up. It would be in your best interest if I dropped the case. Maybe my last act can be saving you from these crooked politicians."

Andrea studied him, empathy and pity pouring from her.

"I think we understand each other. After all, we had this conversation once before. But, Mr. Longbow, I beg you—don't drop the case. Please, give all those other people a chance, a fighting chance. I'll be your general. You and Marcy, God rest her soul, will be the foot soldiers who help me win this war. We'll drive the enemy back behind the lines of big money and backroom deals. This is our chance to make a difference, to get justice for Marcy."

"I don't know," he sighed.

"Can you please just trust me?" Andrea implored.

He rocked twice to create momentum to reach his feet. "Okay, young lady," he grumbled. "It's your funeral."

CHAPTER TEN

Andrea

Michael was true to his word. The two lawyers appeared before Judge Alvin Rubin to argue Michael's Motion for Summary Disposition. Friday was motion day in Wayne County. The courtroom was packed. Attorneys waited impatiently for the judge to decide mundane substantive or procedural issues that could be quickly resolved through diplomacy.

Andrea sat in the gallery, arms folded, increasingly agitated, rolling her eyes at the nonsense. Michael had yet to arrive. *No wonder the docket is crowded. Can't lawyers agree on anything? How does Rubin do this every Friday?*

Rubin's current case involved a litigant's refusal to attend an independent medical examination in an automobile no-fault case.

"I demand that this examination be referred to as a 'defense medical examination,' Your Honor," the plaintiff's lawyer argued.

"The doctor is independent, Your Honor. He has no skin in the game," the defense lawyer retorted.

"How often have you used this doc to examine injured auto accident victims?" Rubin inquired.

"I'm not sure," the defense counsel replied.

"More than ten?" Rubin asked.

"Yes, Your Honor."

"More than fifty?"

"Probably, Your Honor. I'd have to check."

"I will take judicial notice that the defense conducted the examination. I'll give the jury a cautionary instruction. Will that suffice, counsel?" Rubin addressed the plaintiff's attorney.

"Yes, Your Honor."

"Prepare an order for my signature. Next case."

"Ugh," Andrea groaned.

The clerk shouted, "Longbow v. The State of Michigan et al."

"Defense is ready, Your Honor," Michael shouted from behind Andrea, entering the courtroom with an entourage of associates and clerks.

"Plaintiff is ready, Your Honor," Andrea responded, standing at her gallery seat.

"Come forward," the judge ordered. He looked over his reading glasses at the clerk. "Appearances for the record, please?"

"Michael O'Hara, for the Defense, Your Honor."

"Andrea Kramer, for the Plaintiff, Your Honor."

"What's this all about?" Judge Rubin continued to review papers on his desk as if reading the motion for the first time.

"This is my Motion for Summary Disposition, Your Honor," Michael began. "The government has complete immunity in assault cases.

While Plaintiff's daughter's death is tragic, Michigan is protected. The law is clear that—"

"I agree, Your Honor," Andrea interrupted.

The judge smiled and studied Andrea. "That's refreshing, Ms. Kramer. So, why are we here? Why don't I sign an order dismissing this case? Why do I have a feeling you have additional arguments to make?"

"Because you are a wise and experienced jurist, Your Honor. May I continue?"

"You may."

"Wrongful death by assault at the Capitol is only one count of the complaint. The Government cannot assault a citizen. Only people can do that. However, in this case, there are two exceptions to governmental immunity, and we are far too early in the discovery phase of this litigation to determine whether they apply."

"Ms. Kramer, I've read your brief. I'm prepared to rule. For the record, will you please state those exceptions you reference?"

"The two exceptions are gross negligence and government building, Your Honor. The assault on Marcy Longbow happened at the top of the Capitol Steps, just *inside* the building. The government failed to control the crowd, and its leaders planned and participated in the insurrection. They knew or with reasonable care should have known that this riot would cause destruction and serious injury, even death."

"Your Honor—" Michael countered.

"I've heard enough, Mr. O'Hara. I'm prepared to rule," the judge declared. "Your motion is denied. Ms. Kramer is correct that it is far too early in the process for this motion. You may refile later. I must warn you, however, that I am inclined to give Ms. Kramer a chance to prove her case to a jury. Whether or not the building exception can be used in an assault case is not settled law. Moreover, whether the government's conduct rises to gross negligence in this case is a jury question. Eyewitness and expert testimony at trial will be required to make that determination."

"But Your Honor—" Michael pleaded.

"Call the next case," the judge instructed the clerk.

Michael stormed out of the courtroom, closely followed by his entourage. This was his first courtroom battle with Kramer, and he came out the loser.

"You may want to reconsider making an offer on this case, O'Hara. The judge seems to be leaning my way," Andrea rubbed it in as they reached the outer lobby.

He did not turn to face her. "See you at the next deposition, Kramer," Michael grumbled over his shoulder. He shut his briefcase, handed it to an associate, and walked away.

***

Andrea expected Michael to request a series of delays to outlast Mr. Longbow. She pledged to carry on in his stead if anything terrible happened.

"Judge Rubin was correct in the motion ruling, but I'm not sure how we win this at trial," Sheila opined. "There, I said it. Shoot me if you want to, but the law favors immunity for the government. I like the building exception. Marcy's death occurred *inside* the Capitol building, not on the outside steps. You'll probably face endless appeals even if you can convince the jury. O'Hara's client is about as big as it gets."

"Gross negligence also gets us past immunity, but I know we have an uphill climb. While the evidence hasn't come in exactly as I planned, it's still early. We work hard, outsmart, and outmaneuver O'Hara. We locate and depose everyone who was even near the Capitol that day. If this case is so easy to defend, why does the state retain a top firm like Taggert?"

"Because they can *afford* to, using taxpayer dollars! The Taggert firm doesn't have to advance costs. The *citizens* do it for them! The law is the law, for us or against us—firm size doesn't come into play," Sheila insisted.

"Play is correct. This is a courtroom stage with two actors—O'Hara and me. We defeated his SD motion. Unless his client makes a great offer, the case is going to trial. We can each tell our stories and leave it to the jury to decide. Yes, Michael is personable and handsome. The women will swoon, but what about the men? Am I chopped liver? I'll make sure we pick a balanced, representative jury. We've got a better, more compelling story. And Judge Rubin seems to be leaning our way," Andrea concluded.

"So, we want men on the jury? Who wins depends on who has the best play? I'd rather work our collective asses off and prove we have the best *case*," Sheila insisted.

"Amen to that. Shall we get to work?"

The two lawyers bent over their computers, combing LexisNexis and Westlaw for anything related. After what seemed like hours, Andrea excitedly motioned to Sheila. "Got something!"

"What?" Sheila asked.

"Let me read it to you," Andrea replied. "A 2017 news article discusses a wrongful death lawsuit filed against South Carolina for failing to train or supervise prison guards effectively. The state's negligence caused an inmate's death.

"And here's another one: A 2019 report on a two-million-dollar settlement against New York in favor of a group of inmates who sued the state for not providing proper training for correction officers," Andrea continued.

"That's promising. And I found several cases in LexisNexis that involve states being sued for failure to properly train guards, including cases in Idaho, South Carolina, and Pennsylvania," Sheila advised.

"Oh, those are good. Let's dig into those and develop an argument," Andrea exclaimed, buoyed by the fruits of their research.

Sheila nodded and kept reading. "Listen to this one. In a 2012 *Michigan* case, an inmate sued the state for failing to provide appropriate training in a prison. More specifically, the plaintiff claimed that the state violated his constitutional rights by failing to provide adequate training to prison guards on the use of solitary confinement." She turned the monitor toward Andrea.

"The court found that the state had a duty to provide reasonable training to prison guards on the use of solitary confinement and that their failure to do so was a violation of the plaintiff's constitutional rights. The court ultimately ordered the state to pay the plaintiff seventy-five hundred dollars in damages. The case is *Smith v. Michigan Department of Corrections.*" Andrea turned back to Sheila.

"I think we've hit gold. We know our angle. But can we overcome immunity? Can inadequate training reach the level of *gross* negligence?" Sheila addressed a crucial issue in the case.

"In addition to our alternate viable theories, I believe it can. Why did the various states pay in those cases? They *had* to reach the required level or avoid immunity. What do *you* think?" Andrea inquired.

Sheila's disposition brightened, "I'm on it."

Michael

"I need settlement authority, Stu! We're going to lose this case!"

"Calm down, Michael. You've tried more cases than your young opponent. You've got a solid governmental immunity argument. Try the case and kick her ass," Taggert advised.

"How's the view from the expensive seats, Stu? When was the last case you tried?" Michael snarled.

"I don't like your tone, O'Hara. Watch yourself."

"I'm sorry," Michael calmed. "Cheap shot, but it doesn't change things. We are going to get hit big on this case. Immunity aside, public sentiment and the press are against us. The law is iffy and can go both ways. There is ample precedent. We lost the summary disposition motion. Kramer may prevail on gross negligence.

"It's *Rinke*, Stu! He's a crazy fuck! He's nowhere to be found, and he was *governor* when he gave that speech. I need authority to settle."

"AG Wallace is a brick wall, Michael. I told you this the other ten times you asked for settlement authority. Wallace won't even renew the original offer."

"Why, Stu? His stubbornness is going to cost the taxpayers millions."

"The truth?" Taggert turned and stared out the window.

"Nothing but," Michael studied his boss.

"It's political. He and Grimes are Dems. Rinke's a Rhino. A large verdict would reflect poorly on the Republican Party."

"Wallace *told* you that?"

"Of course not, Michael. He's an intelligent guy, a politician's politician. He would never admit that."

"Where does that leave me?"

"You're the scapegoat, son. Your only chance is to win the case. I'm sorry."

"You're *sorry*? This is my *career* we're talking about. What about the partnership?"

"Lose the case, and you lose more than the partnership, Michael."

"I can't believe I let you do this to me. You're an asshole."

"Yes, I am, but I'm the senior partner. I'm paid to be an asshole."

CHAPTER ELEVEN

TRIAL

Andrea

Andrea stood on the McArthur Bridge leading to Belle Isle. Face to the wind, hypnotized by rushing water, she focused on life amidst the concrete, lies, and evil that permeated her world. She grounded herself, attempting to push out the negative and pull in the positive. She inhaled the smell of fresh-cut grass, scanned the blue waters, and watched the ducks wander along the bank.

The night before, Andrea and Sheila completed their research and developed a comprehensive trial brief. Andrea wrote a compelling opening statement with indexed trial exhibits, deposition transcripts, and other discovery documents, highlighted testimonial inconsistencies, and practiced examination and cross-examination techniques.

Andrea was confident but cautious, determined but nervous. What would matter more, politics or the law? She slapped the bridge rail with her palm and resolved to obtain justice to the best of her ability. She drove to the courthouse, focused on the task ahead. Neither the morning rush nor the inevitable difficulty locating a parking space would deter her.

Andrea entered the courthouse, displayed her bar card, and sailed through security. She stood in the hallway outside Judge Alvin Rubin's courtroom, hoping to see Mr. Longbow. Each upper floor in the building houses four circuit court judges. Thus, the hallway was packed with attorneys and citizens waiting for the sixteenth-floor jurists to dispense justice.

Sheila wandered over, shaking her head. "I can't find him. He's not answering his cell."

Andrea ignored her, determined to remain positive. "If necessary, Rubin will grant an adjournment."

"Of course, if necessary, but it won't be . . . necessary, I mean. He'll show up. Not to worry." Sheila looked plenty worried. A door behind them banged open, and a court officer appeared.

"The court is open for business," he declared.

Andrea and Sheila walked into the courtroom and stood in a short line of attorneys waiting to check in for pre-trials and other preliminary matters or have the judge read and sign an order. Andrea checked in with the court clerk, walked to the plaintiff's table on the right, and sat.

A line of chairs behind her was filled with attorneys, waiting for Judge Rubin to attend to the everyday, mundane matters handled in circuit court. As Andrea waited, she became nervous. She fidgeted, busied herself, and tested the microphone for sound. She organized and laid out file contents, *voir dire* questions, and a draft of her opening statement. Finally, she reviewed bookmarks and indexed deposition transcripts, exhibits, photos, and other material she would rely upon to present her case.

She sensed a presence pass behind her and to her left. She glanced up and looked over her left shoulder. Michael O'Hara and his entourage arrived at the defense table.

Looking less confident than usual, Michael nodded to Andrea and glanced at the bench and jury box. Perhaps he envisioned the captivating arguments he would soon make to the judge and jury. He walked over to the plaintiff's table.

"Good morning. All set to do battle?"

"Ready as I'll ever be," she replied.

"Whatever happens, I want you to know that it has been a pleasure working with you on this case and getting to know you. You have done a terrific job for your client. If the AG's office wasn't so stingy, we might have settled this and become friends."

"Friends?" Andrea chuckled. "We're from two different worlds. How about we advance to 'frenemies?'"

"I don't know, I enjoyed my time in Saline. I might consider a small-town practice somewhere down the road."

Andrea laughed and pointed out the window. "Way down the road."

"Maybe sooner than that," Michael warned. "Let's see what happens. Good luck to you and your unfortunate client, whatever the outcome."

"Thank you, Michael. That's kind of you. Good luck in your future endeavors . . . *after* the Longbow case."

Michael chuckled. "Thank you. Speaking about after the Longbow case, if I am ever out your way . . . Saline or maybe Ann Arbor . . . might we get together for coffee or lunch?"

"I don't see why not," Andrea agreed, immediately regretting her words.

The legal combatants returned to their respective clients and files. Andrea smiled to herself and peeked at Michael. *He is so cocky . . . but for a good reason.* Michael and his team did an admirable job. A brilliant discovery strategy, and their trial brief read like a compelling legal thriller. Evidence development and legal arguments were solid. Probing deposition questions tainted Andrea's best experts and eyewitnesses. He was a formidable adversary, the most talented lawyer she ever faced. If she didn't have the truth on her side—

He's not just a pretty face. She learned a lot working with Michael and his team during the pre-trial phase of the case. Would she be attracted to him if he wasn't her courtroom opponent? *Some other time . . . some other place?*

Pre-trial preparation is vital to success, but it isn't everything. Overconfidence is quite dangerous in court. Underestimating your opponent, not recognizing a judge's or juror's nuances, or displaying too much attitude in front of the jury could easily derail your case.

It may work for him. He's a successful litigator. He had his style—she had hers. *Let the jury decide based on the evidence, not the defense lawyer's looks or confident nature.*

Andrea sensed another presence, this time to her right. She again glanced up. Mr. Longbow stood next to her, gripping the handle of a walking stick with one hand, leaning on the back of her chair with the other. He was pale, and his chin quivered. Tethered to a tank behind him, a cannula was tucked into his nose.

Someone came with him—a good friend? *Perhaps she's a nurse.* Longbow shot Andrea a questioning look, and she nodded at the chair next to her own. He all but fell into the chair. His physical condition had deteriorated since they were last together. Aside from the oxygen tank, he'd lost weight, appeared unkempt, and was so emaciated he could hardly walk or stand. Even seated, he looked to be in great pain.

"Are you okay? I was afraid you wouldn't make it." Andrea immediately winced at her choice of words.

"I wasn't sure either. I know, I look like death warmed over. Let's not waste energy talking about me. Let's get this done. Who are all these people?" He looked around the packed courtroom, taking in the unknown faces, trying to recognize someone.

"The judge has a lot of preliminary matters to dispose of before he gets to ours. We'll have to wait for him to attend to those before he gets to our case," Andrea explained.

"Why doesn't he schedule the trial after the preliminary stuff?" Longbow reasoned.

Andrea chuckled at the common-sense suggestion. "That makes too much sense. In the law biz, we call this practice ritual 'hurry up and wait.' The judge calls us in early because he'd rather we wait for him than vice versa."

"Well, that's tough—he'll have to wait for me."

Andrea frowned, not sure what he meant and unwilling to ask. She hoped he didn't plan to use the trial to grandstand, protest, or perhaps engage in some hateful rebellion against the world. She didn't know him well but presumed he was smart enough to appreciate that a court of law was inappropriate for such nonsense.

Michael

Michael O'Hara was still reeling from his showdown with Taggert. He studied Andrea as she conversed with her client. Longbow seemed agitated. *What's the problem, Mr. Longbow? She's done a terrific job for you. She's winning your case!*

Andrea Kramer proved to be more than a worthy opponent. *She's a tremendous advocate, brilliant, and a stunningly beautiful woman. Under different circumstances—*

"All rise! Circuit court for the county of Wayne is now in session. The Honorable Judge Alvin Rubin presiding. Those with matters before the court, please step forward," the bailiff shouted. He didn't expect an avalanche of people to step forward at once. This was a term of expression to advise the lawyers to get ready to be heard.

Cases were called, one by one, disposed of by a private discussion in chambers, a short hearing on the record, or a simple presentation of documents for the judge to read and sign or refuse to sign for various reasons.

Two hours later, the courtroom had cleared out. Aside from court personnel, Andrea, Sheila, Longbow, Michael, and his entourage of clerks and grunts were the only people in the room.

"Call the case of Longbow v. State of Michigan," the clerk screeched.

Judge Rubin assumed the bench, nodded at the lawyers and litigants, and tapped his microphone.

"This is the date and date scheduled for the trial. Are there preliminary matters to discuss before I bring in the jury panel?"

There were numerous motions and legal maneuvers. Both sides wanted specific evidence and potential testimony excluded or admitted. Michael renewed his dispositive motion and was shot down by Rubin. The judge showed incredible patience, listening to the arguments of both sides of each issue. In the end, his rulings were almost fifty-fifty, with a slight edge to the plaintiff. The legal mumbo-jumbo took about an hour and a half.

"Anything else?" Judge Rubin inquired.

"No, Your Honor," the two lawyers stood and responded in unison.

"Bring in the jury panel, please."

The clerk left the courtroom and returned with sixty jurors. As the panel shuffled about, trying to get comfortable, the women looked around, wondering whether they should hold their purses or set them on the floor at the risk of having them fall over. Andrea studied the jurors, wondering whether more information could be learned about their character by going through purses or wallets, emptying pockets, or scanning cellphones rather than asking probing questions to determine their biases.

Judge Rubin conducted *voir dire*. If the attorneys were lucky, he might permit them a few questions. The jurors were instructed to rise and raise their right hands. The clerk administered an oath for jurors to promise to answer challenge questions truthfully.

"Ladies and gentlemen, thank you for your service. Trials are not possible without unbiased citizens willing to drop everything and participate for a day, a week, sometimes even weeks or months, to be part of our justice system.

"I want to remind you that this is *not* a criminal case. It is a civil case where you will be called upon to determine liability and damages. It concerns an event that has been in the news: the protest at the Capitol, a clash between protestors and the police that resulted in some injuries and one unfortunate death.

"Former Governor Gordon Rinke, who did not participate in the protest, is accused of inciting the resulting violence. Because he was governor of Michigan at the time, one of the issues you will be determining is whether he was acting as governor, as a candidate for office, or both."

The judge continued. "Have you read or heard anything about this case or any litigants?"

Every hand in the panel shot up.

"Silly question. Of *course,* you have."

"Your Honor, at this time, we renew our motion for a change of venue," O'Hara stood and demanded.

"Ms. Kramer?" The judge invited Andrea to respond.

Andrea

"Your honor, everyone in Michigan has read or heard something about this incident." Andrea was careful not to use the word 'insurrection.'

"The issue is whether what they read or heard will affect their ability to be fair and impartial. Counsel has already requested and received a venue change to this honorable court. This is not Ingham County, where the events in question occurred."

"I quite agree, Ms. Kramer. Mr. O'Hara, your motion is denied. You may renew it if the jury selection process does not ferret things out."

Other issues were addressed and handled. Jurors were excused for various reasons. New jurors were summoned in their places and asked the same questions as their predecessors.

Juror number fifteen was thanked and excused because of a prior criminal conviction. Juror thirty-two worked for the federal government. Juror forty-six was dismissed because the DEA raided his house the day before and found a large stash of drugs. And Juror fifty-seven was disqualified because she once worked for the state.

The judge asked whether any member of the jury panel, immediate family members, or close personal friends had ever made claims in the legal system, even if they did not go to trial.

A prospective juror stood and raised his hand.

"Yes, sir. Please step up to the podium," the judge ordered. The man did as he was instructed.

"Your juror number, please?" asked the clerk.

"Seven." The man leaned forward to speak into the microphone. It squealed loudly, causing everyone in the courtroom to recoil.

"You don't need to get that close to the mike to be heard," the judge politely advised.

"Sorry, Your Honor."

"Please tell us about your experience," the judge requested.

The man moved his face a bit further from the microphone. "It was a slip and fall accident at Kroger four or five years ago."

"Did you file a lawsuit?"

"I don't know. I hired one of those lawyers on TV. One of his people handled everything."

"What was the result of the case?"

"They gave me five thousand dollars."

"And that was here in Wayne County?"

"Yes, Your Honor."

"Were you satisfied with the results of the case? No hard feelings?"

"Oh, yes. I sprained my wrist and wrenched my back."

"In light of that experience, do you feel you can be a fair and impartial juror in *this* case?" the judge asked.

"I . . . I think I can serve as a juror."

"You hesitated. Can you unequivocally state that you can be fair and impartial?"

"I don't know what that means."

"What?"

"Unequivla . . ."

"Unequivocal means 'for sure.'"

"Well, Your Honor, I'm not sure about that."

"You believe your experience with Kroger might carry over to this case?"

"Yes, sir."

"Okay. I understand."

"Because of all the pain and suffering I've had to deal with," he exaggerated. It became apparent that this man did not wish to serve on the jury.

"We're going to thank and excuse you from this trial. Stick around, though. We'll try to seat you for a criminal case or a dispute that doesn't involve an injury or death." The judge knew what the man was up to and called his bluff. Juror number seven would sit in court all day, waiting to be assigned.

The selection exercise continued back and forth between the jurors, Judge Rubin, and the two attorneys. One juror worked for a lawyer who did not handle personal injury cases. One juror's nephew was an attorney. Another was a public defender—he was excused.

"Do any jurors work in or have close relatives or personal friends who work in law enforcement?"

One juror was a cop. Another had a brother who was a Michigan State Trooper. They were both thanked and excused. Several more testified that they had served on juries before.

"Does any jury panel member have any preconceived notions, prejudices, or feelings about people who bring lawsuits or make claims for injuries? Does anyone feel positive or negative about insurance companies or other people who defend these cases?" The judge inquired. The panel was silent.

The judge was thorough and eventually gave the attorneys latitude to ask questions. It was a tedious but necessary process. A fair and impartial jury, selected by both sides of a legal dispute, is the cornerstone of a fair trial. Seven jurors made the final cut: four men and three women. One of those would become an alternate, dismissed if not needed for deliberations.

When jury selection was finally over, the seven citizens filed in and were seated in pre-selected spots. Michael renewed his motion for a change of venue. Judge Rubin denied the motion, and the clerk swore in the jury.

"Do you solemnly promise and declare that you will try the issues before you and render a true, fair, and impartial verdict based solely upon the evidence?"

The jurors promised. The judge briefed the panel about opening statements and other procedural matters.

"During the trial or recess, do not express opinions to your fellow jurors about the case. Please do not even discuss the matter amongst yourselves or with others. Don't even allow yourself to overhear *anyone* talking about it. Base your decision only on the evidence presented in this courtroom.

"Please keep an open mind throughout these proceedings. After you've heard the lawyers' opening statements, all the evidence, and the lawyers' closing arguments at the end of the case, I will explain the law that applies to this case. Understood?"

The jurors nodded.

"I will now invite the attorneys to deliver opening statements. Ms. Kramer?"

"Thank you, Your Honor." Andrea rose and strolled to the podium.

She adjusted the podium to face the jury and began her opening.

"Ladies and gentlemen of the jury, thank you for your service. On November 8, 2022, Michigan held an election. Gordon Rinke, the Republican incumbent, was challenged by Charlie Page, now Governor Page, a Democrat. According to all election officials, reporters, and two unnecessary but expensive recounts, Page handily won the election.

"A complete discussion of the issues, a fair election, and a public repudiation of his policies and demeanor was not enough for Gordon Rinke. He used his office and taxpayer dollars to declare that the election was ripe with corruption and fraud.

"Had Gordon Rinke stopped there, with false allegations of fraud costing the taxpayers millions in recount dollars, we would not be here today, and a young woman would not have tragically lost her life. But he wouldn't stop.

"On November 21, 2022, Gordon Rinke assembled a mob. He spoke from his bully pulpit, still in his capacity as Michigan's governor, and declared that he won the election. He called the 2022 election "the most corrupt election in American history."

"Again, ladies and gentlemen, if he was only guilty of lying about the election results and vote tabulations, we would not be here today. So, you may ask, why *are* we here? Isn't free speech the cornerstone of our democracy?

"Yes, free speech is a precious constitutional right in America, so precious, our forefathers drafted the First Amendment to the United States Constitution to preserve it. However, the right to free speech is not unlimited. A citizen, especially the governor of one of our fifty states, may not yell "fire" in a crowded theater without being responsible for the consequences.

"In this case, Governor Rinke, acting in his official capacity as governor, yelled "fire!" Here's the video of his speech to his angry supporters, dangerous people who the governor knew would do his bidding."

A computer and a large screen were set up in the center of the courtroom. A young clerk stepped forward and played a video of Rinke's speech. When the recording ended, Andrea paused. She wanted the video to sink in, for the jury to consider Rinke's words and hold them against him. After what she regarded as sufficient time, she continued.

"Governor Rinke is a coward," Andrea grumbled. "He was not brave enough to lead his assembled mob into the Capitol. He is not brave enough to appear before you today. But he lit a fuse that invited violence—you heard his words. When his speech ended, his security team whisked this coward to safety while his angry supporters descended on the Capitol screaming, "Stop the steal." Police erected barricades at the bottom and top of the Capitol steps and formed defensive lines to prevent a breach of the building.

"Their numbers were grossly insufficient to cover the entire building. Aside from Rinke's outrageous and deliberate behavior, we intend to show that the state was grossly negligent in mounting its defense of the Capitol. The size and quality of the response was woefully inadequate. The media warned that this event was potentially dangerous, even catastrophic, yet Rinke's government ignored all warnings," Andrea charged.

"All the protestors needed to do was advance on the opposite side of the building. Armed with assault rifles, this smaller group easily breached the inadequately guarded back entrances. The back entrance protestors raced through the lobby and headed toward the front entrance. When they arrived, they rushed through the panic doors behind the officers and pushed the helpless officers down the stairs. They kicked down the barriers from behind.

"When that happened, ladies and gentlemen, the larger group watched and laughed as brave, dedicated but overmatched officers rolled past them down the Capitol steps. Anarchists could now and did breach the main entrance. While state representatives and senators were evacuated before the speech, administrative staff members and the public were in grave danger, left to their own devices in the face of an angry mob. Here's another video of *these* events."

Again, the young clerk stepped forward and played a graphic video, which displayed the events as Andrea described them. She paused to study the jurors' faces. *I'm connecting.* They're *listening.* She continued with confidence.

"The Capitol riots lasted *three hours* before the building was secured, ladies and gentlemen. Governor Gordon Rinke, the man who inspired the riot and yelled "fire" in a crowded theater, ran like a coward and could not be found.

"The Capitol building suffered millions in property and artifact damage. Many officers and citizens were injured, some seriously injured, and sadly, a solitary citizen was killed. Just inside the building, my client's daughter, Marcy Longbow, was trampled to death by a stampeding mob.

"Marcy was an outstanding student, worked through school, spent two years at Lansing Community College, and transferred to Michigan State University, earning a bachelor's degree in public administration.

"She was a hard worker, a fine person, loved by her father, friends, and co-workers. You will hear from many of these people. Marcy did charity work at Sparrow Hospital. She believed in democracy and our justice system, supporting causes that protected the most vulnerable members of our society. That's why she chose to major in public administration. She wanted to make a difference."

Andrea spoke about Arthur Longbow's personal survivor loss case, smiled at the jurors, and sat down. Longbow was in tears. Andrea patted his hand and glanced at the jury. All eyes were upon the lawyer and her client.

Michael's opening statement was less dynamic and far less emotional. He argued that Rinke's speech was political, not gubernatorial, and not an official speech on behalf of the state. As such, it was not the exercise of an official government function.

"There is not a shred of evidence to prove that Governor Rinke was acting in his official capacity, rather than as a private citizen—a former candidate for office." This argument was Andrea's biggest fear. The state might not be liable unless Rinke was engaged in a government function.

The trial lasted two weeks. Dozens of witnesses testified under oath, including right-wing election deniers who suddenly came to Jesus after learning they could face severe criminal penalties. Witness after witness testified that they would be spending time in prison or on probation because Gordon Rinke, the duly elected governor of Michigan, *ordered* them to storm the Capitol building.

Capitol Police officers and innocent citizens who showed up expecting a peaceful protest testified to the brutality of the rioters, the various beatings they incurred, and the severe, life-altering injuries they suffered. Television news personalities testified to the accuracy of Andrea's video evidence presentation.

Michael objected to these videos, arguing they were too graphic and tainted the jury. "Prejudice outweighs probative value," he reasoned.

Judge Rubin overruled his objections, indicating that conditions leading up to and including the riot were "absolutely relevant" to the case and outweighed possible prejudice to the defendants.

Aside from the graphic video evidence, Arthur Longbow's testimony was the most compelling evidence at trial. He testified to the character, potential, personality, and youthful exuberance of Marcy Longbow. He tearfully described her joyful presence and how much he would miss this treasured human being.

While others testified to witnessing her pain, suffering, slow, terrible, and brutal death, Longbow testified to her *spirit* and the emptiness of all who knew and missed her, thanks to Rinke, his followers, and a government that callously refused to rein in these criminals. The rioters were unbelievably cruel. Their brutality was savage, and Andrea presented it all on video.

Michael tried his best to counter Andrea's powerful presentation of the graphic video evidence. There is an old saying among trial lawyers that goes something like this: "If you have the facts on your side, argue the facts. If you have the law on your side, argue the law. If you have neither on your side, pound the table."

Michael O'Hara spent two weeks pounding the table. Andrea not only had the better case; she worked harder and tried a better case than the talented and experienced O'Hara. When it was over, the jury deliberated for four days. Jurors unanimously held Gordon Rinke and the government responsible for the wrongful death and pain and suffering of Marcy Longbow. They rendered an eight-figure joint and several damages award.

In a now-empty courtroom, Andrea and Sheila packed their files and evidence materials into briefcases and file boxes. Michael approached the table, chin high as always, and held out his hand. "Congratulations on a job well done."

She grabbed the handle of her mobile file transport carrier and looked up at him. "Thank you. This was a tough case, but the evidence was hard to overcome, even for you. It's impossible to derail a speeding freight train of evidence."

"In this business, you play the hand you're dealt. You win some and lose some. I'll be back," he replied with his best impression of Arnold Schwarzenegger.

Andrea laughed. "This was a compelling case. I've had my share of turkeys and losers. I'll lose my share in the future. The stars were aligned for this one."

"Don't diminish what you've done."

"I'm not. I warned you. You should have settled this case when you had the chance. The evidence was compelling."

"My hands were tied. Still, I might have beaten a less worthy opponent. You did a brilliant job and should be proud of the work you did for your client."

"Thank you again. I *am* proud. More important, though, I am happy for *him*." Andrea's eyes moved away from Michael's ashen face and into the face of the older man standing behind him.

Longbow was still tearful, cannula in place, looking weaker than when he entered the courtroom two weeks ago, leaning heavily on his cane.

"The state of Michigan didn't cause his daughter's death. We will be appealing," Michael promised.

"This was a clean trial. I don't see the court of appeals overturning this verdict," Andrea predicted.

"We'll see." The smile was gone. Michael walked up to Longbow and congratulated him.

"I'm sorry for your loss, sir. Marcy was a wonderful person. Congratulations on a hard-fought victory." He held out his hand to Longbow, who refused to shake it.

"Why would you defend a case like this? In my culture, we call this defending the indefensible," he grumbled.

"I work for a law firm. I'm required to defend the cases and clients my superiors assign to me. That doesn't mean I'm always happy or agree with them. That's the business. When you work for others, you don't get to choose."

"I suppose. May God forgive you."

For the first time Andrea could remember, Michael O'Hara hung his head. He gave Andrea a quarter wave, nodded at Longbow, and turned to walk out of the courtroom.

Andrea appreciated Michael's post-trial contrition, especially his words to Longbow. She felt almost *sorry* for him.

"Michael? Don't forget. If you're out my way—"

"I may take you up on that," he retorted, a thin smile crossing his lips.

Andrea and Sheila walked Longbow out and summoned a taxi.

"Is this over?" Longbow wondered. "When will we receive the award? It's blood money, you know. I plan to donate it to charity."

"We're far from seeing anyone write a check, Mr. Longbow. The hard part is done. In the future, you won't have to do anything unless the court of appeals grants a new trial, and we must do this all over again.

"They will appeal. You can count on that. It will take a year or two, at least. I believe we will prevail. Judge Rubin did a good job—I don't see any issues that would result in a successful appeal. Letting in the video evidence was entirely within his discretion. We'll have to wait out the process," Andrea concluded.

"I'm not sure how much time I have left."

"We can plan with a will or a trust. See me at the office and we'll discuss things. For now, we've won the case. I know this is a bittersweet occasion, and I won't be able to coax a smile out of you. Can we, at least, savor the victory? We can't bring Marcy back, but it's a good day for justice," she encouraged.

Longbow looked heartbroken, in more pain than the day he walked into her office all those months ago. She watched as Sheila helped him into the cab and waved as he drove away.

Judge Rubin sent a law student, the young clerk who played the videos, to help the two women lug their files to a nearby parking garage. The kid walked the carrier and carried a large box in his other hand. Sheila and Andrea each had a few files, but the kid assumed the bulk of the burden. He followed them to their cars.

Andrea opened her trunk. The clerk carefully placed the folders, exhibits, and boxes inside. He folded the carrier, put it on top, and shut the trunk.

"Will there be anything else?" he asked Andrea.

"No, thanks. You've been a big help." She tried to hand him a five-dollar bill, but he waved it away. She persisted, but he backed up, refusing the cash.

"I don't want your money. These last two weeks were amazing! It was a pleasure to watch you try that case. I've never seen anything like it. I'm a third-year student at the University of Detroit Law School. My internship with Judge Rubin is almost finished. Would it be possible for me to clerk in your office? Follow your trials? You won't have to pay me. I'd be honored to have you as a mentor."

Andrea smiled. "Thanks for the kind words. My practice is in Saline, near Ann Arbor. You're welcome anytime. Drive through town. Look for a converted barn and silo with my name on the door. You can't miss it. Come in—say hello."

He laughed. "I'll do that."

"I'm not sure about the logistics, but I'd be happy to have you clerk a few days a week. I might even be able to pay you if this case ever resolves," she smiled.

"Thank you. It will be worth a drive to Saline."

CHAPTER TWELVE

Michael

"The trial was the disaster of disasters, a fiasco, Michael!" Attorney General Wallace raged, a look of pure fury on his face.

"You let us down, big time. You botched this thing from beginning to end and got your ass kicked by a rookie. After the appeals are exhausted, assuming they go the way I expect, the taxpayers will pay a high price for your trial errors and general incompetence."

Michael remained silent, seething, slowly reaching a boiling point. *Damn you! I told you to settle! Politics, my ass!* Andrea uncovered a veritable treasure trove of evidence and relevant case law to defeat immunity. Why wouldn't the government offer mediation or a substantial settlement to a dying man? *Politics!*

Andrea effectively utilized available discovery tools and did a brilliant job locating witnesses and compiling documentary evidence. She carefully developed witnesses and expertly deposed them. She won most of the pre-trial motions, including every dispositive motion. *I warned you!* Stu

Taggert and AG Wallace ignored every warning—this huge loss lay at their doorstep.

He shut his mouth and took the criticism. Waves of embarrassment and anger continued to pulsate through him. He worked his ass off on a case he couldn't win. His solid advice was ignored. Instead, the AG doubled down, first yanking the original offer and then refusing to consider *any* offer during discovery or trial, even after it became clear they were losing.

Now, Taggert and the AG needed to deflect blame. They needed a scapegoat. They planned this from the beginning. *It's all O'Hara's fault. He had an excellent track record. Who could expect him to be so incompetent?*

Behind Wallace's back, Michael and Stu Taggert reached a secret agreement. Michael was offered and accepted an unprecedented eight-figure severance package and an NDA in exchange for a promise never to discuss the circumstances of his termination. Taggert, who hired and mentored O'Hara, kicked him to the curb.

"I had no choice," Stu argued.

"You had plenty of choices. You chose the political gutter. I wish you nothing but the worst," Michael retorted.

"Don't forget," Taggert warned. "The NDA goes both ways. We will not bad mouth you; you're walking away a wealthy man. You can choose your own path. I know you're angry—I don't blame you. You've had a lot of success here—often did brilliant work and made the firm a ton of money. You'll land on your feet."

You made me take this case! You assigned it to me to keep from getting your ass kicked. Gutless prick! I was your hand-picked scapegoat from the beginning.

Michael nodded wordlessly, jaw tight, angry as hell, embarrassed for some reason. He knew this was coming, but it still stung. Termination was often the price of failure in the legal profession. *What's become of loyalty? Screw this! Their loss will be another firm's gain. I'll achieve success elsewhere—throw their mistake in their collective faces.*

He packed up his office and strolled out, head down, humiliated to be escorted out by security in front of the entire office.

Taggert was right about one thing. When Michael first accepted the case, he assumed he would beat Andrea. He was late doing his homework. He misjudged the sheer volume of evidence and his opponent's ability to use it. He worked hard and expected to prevail. Sometimes, however, the deck is stacked against you.

His most important lessons? He learned to be a graceful and humble loser. The law was a *business*, not some altruistic calling. When a mentor must choose between covering his ass or protecting his first mate, he'll cover his ass every single time.

From this moment forward, Michael O'Hara would count only on himself. He would use his anger, frustration, and humiliation as fuel to become a better lawyer. He would never again put his fate in someone else's hands. He hated losing—it wasn't part of his DNA. He loved winning and winners . . . *Andrea* . . . She was all he could think about as security escorted him out of the building.

Michael walked to a local tavern. He got seriously drunk, not his usual one-night binge, but a multi-night adventure in heavy drinking. He was not accustomed to failure. It hit him hard.

The O'Hara family was wealthy, powerful, and *connected*. His career success came, at least in part, from those connections. Family donations to the university's law library secured his admission to a prestigious law school. Taggert, Miles, & Freeman was Michael's first job out of law school, made possible by his father's connections with the senior partner of the silk-stocking law firm in Detroit.

Michael's success was not all smoke and mirrors. He did well in law school, passed the bar on the first try, and did superior legal work for the firm. However, at the dawn of his first partnership opportunity, Stu Taggert dumped the Longbow litigation on him, and hell froze over.

Andrea

While Michael drowned his sorrows in booze, Andrea became the media's new darling. Publicity from the trial, interviews, and accolades from the press resulted in her office becoming extremely busy. Before the Longbow verdict, she waited for the phone to ring, twiddled her thumbs, and readied her new office. Calls involved frivolous legal questions, minor traffic cases, minor judicial assignments, or favors for friends or family members.

Now, after securing a loan from a local bank, the phone rang constantly, answered by a receptionist. Clients inquired about quality cases. Calls were turned over to Andrea, her new associate, or their part-time litigation paralegal, the young intern from Judge Rubin's courtroom who helped carry her trial exhibits to the car.

Andrea earned her success the hard way, going to law school, working for others, hanging her shingle, having the guts to take on a controversial case against an established firm, and working her ass off to best a fine young trial lawyer.

Over the next several months, appeals wound their way through the court system. To this point, she'd won every one of them. The state and the Taggert firm filed their final appeal to the Michigan Supreme Court, arguing that Judge Rubin abused his discretion in allowing certain witnesses to testify and permitting the jury to view the unedited video.

Andrea fully expected that the final appeal would be denied. Quite soon, she would be an even *more* famous local lawyer and a multi-millionaire.

"I don't crave money, Sheila. I crave *freedom.*" Andrea and Sheila were in the office late, discussing the future and drinking stale coffee.

"Money's nice too, Andrea. With money, you can *buy* freedom."

"What do you mean?" Andrea wondered.

"Do you want to do pro-bono work?" Sheila asked.

"Yes."

"Money gives you independence. You can take pro-bono work, right wrongs, donate to charity, use your newfound wealth and power to help people who might not otherwise have access to the justice system," Sheila explained.

Andrea paused, taking in Sheila's words. "The money would also keep my humble legal abode open, sordid history and funny smell aside," she replied.

"Look around you, Andrea. This office is symbolic of *you*, a phoenix rising from the ashes. You *will* win the appeal. You *will* reap the rewards of victory, professional success, and a boatload of money. Don't forget me, but it's time for me to move on."

To Andrea's chagrin, Sheila had decided to return to her life and career. She considered her time with Andrea a wonderful experience and a wise investment.

"There's a place for you here," Andrea protested. "We're busy. I need the help."

"I appreciate the offer and all you've done for me. But I need to forge my path," Sheila determined.

"I understand. I'll miss you," Andrea's voice cracked, tears in her eyes.

"I'll be around. We'll keep in touch. Call me whenever you need me—I'll be there," Sheila promised.

"I will hold you to that."

After Sheila left, Andrea sat in her office and closed her eyes. Her thoughts floated to the day following the Longbow verdict. She pulled the shades, locked the door, and lost herself in a world of self-indulgence for a solid week.

She watched cheesy love stories on the Hallmark Channel, taught herself to crochet, and painted her bedroom. She shopped at thrift stores for furnishings, attempting to make her apartment feel more like a home.

However, at night, when she lay in bed, trying to sleep, her thoughts returned to a dark-haired, silver-tongued, blue-eyed cocky lawyer named Michael O'Hara. O'Hara kept her awake. She heard he left the Taggert firm. Taggert's appellate division handled the appeal. She checked the Michigan Bar Journal Directory to see where he landed, but a post office box was his listed address.

The months after the verdict were Andrea's 'rediscovery months.' The Longbow trial verdict made her a star and caused her to consider the future. Fame cost her privacy. Being a public rebel, champion of the underdog, came at the price of freedom that accompanies anonymity.

Now a hot commodity, Andrea could not leave her office without being accosted by a citizen looking for free legal advice or a media type looking for a sound bite. She became the property of others and lost a bit of herself in the process.

The Michael experience left her dinged. She struggled with feelings she did not know she had until they parted ways. Had they met under different circumstances, not as courtroom gladiators but as neighbors or people introduced at a party, she might have searched for his more admirable qualities. She admired his tenacity and confidence, essential traits for a trial lawyer. His sharp wit and humor annoyed her as his opponent but made her smile as she flashed back. His toned body, six-foot-plus height, dazzling smile, and sky-blue eyes were to die for.

The way he behaved at the Saline tavern when Homer Dunlop walked in with stuff on his shoes, Michael sniffing the air, talking about the quality of the air in the place, was classic, a hysterical round hole/square peg memory she planned to share with friends and family for decades.

She patted herself on the back for ignoring her growing interest and using his attitude as a harpoon to destroy him in front of the jury. At the same time, she felt terrible. The evidence was overwhelming. She had little reason to make it personal. Perhaps she'd make it up to him someday.

Before the trial, she did a Google search on Michael. He came from old money—his family was connected. That's probably how he developed his superior confidence.

Andrea could not understand her feelings. She hardly knew him outside the courtroom. Throughout college and law school, she was always careful around men, especially those in her male-dominated profession. Yet, here she was, post-trial, still struggling with the aftereffects of meeting and beating Michael.

She'd always made it a point not to become involved with a man. In college and law school, she avoided parties, blind dates, and well-intentioned friends who wanted her to lead a less lonely life. While they viewed her as lonely, she considered herself dedicated.

Still, her school years were spent mostly alone. Her arms wrapped around books on Friday and Saturday nights instead of sturdy, attractive college boys. She convinced herself this was how she wanted things, but her inner self screamed: *"Liar!"*

The pragmatic Andrea turned to law school with an obsessive attitude toward self-denial, lofty intentions, and righting social justice wrongs. No man, at least none in her college years, could or would want to accompany her into that world.

Andrea now sought a relationship, not necessarily intimate, but a union of equals, a man who could share her passion for justice. The more she dwelled on the subject, the more she wished to locate Michael O'Hara.

CHAPTER THIRTEEN

Michael

While Andrea Kramer embraced self-discovery, Michael O'Hara embraced self-*destruction*. The money was nice, but Michael shuddered at the realization that one rookie lawyer from a small town near Ann Arbor managed to undo everything he and his family had worked to build since the day he was born.

His parents left him alone to resolve his feelings and sort through the ramifications of his trial loss and termination from the Taggert firm. Michael needed to decide whether and where he wanted to practice law or ask for their help to determine his new career path. He steadfastly refused his father's offer to square things with Taggert.

"I have an NDA, Dad. I can't talk about it. The bottom line is that I won't work for disloyal people."

The cruel media enjoyed his demise, shining a bright spotlight on Andrea, making insinuations about his character, and referring to him as a playboy lawyer. The more they piled on, the moodier and angrier he became. His fury began to fuel every action.

He drank heavily, traveling from bar to bar. Driving while intoxicated—daring the police to flag him for drunk driving—he didn't care about anyone or anything. He hurled insults at bar patrons, got into fistfights, and was thrown out of most establishments he frequented. He was in a dark place, trying to escape the shame of his most impactful professional loss.

Michael met Sarah at one of the bars. The young woman was kind and understanding, the only person who saw the pain behind his arrogant, bombastic, and self-loathing behavior. She tried to draw out his vulnerable side, the deeply pained, flawed, self-flagellating Michael O'Hara. She tried to connect with him, but his pride and anger caused him to reject her unstated offer. Still, she fought hard to redeem his tortured soul.

Despite Michael's drinking and intense fury, the couple enjoyed moments of clarity. Michael was clever, funny, and highly intelligent. He'd share stories about his storied career before the Longbow case ended his string of high-profile professional successes—before the alcohol kicked into gear and turned him into someone his better self would not recognize. While Sarah did not know him during his successful period, she was not surprised by the stories because he was a man far superior to a drunken bar brawler.

"Michael, can we talk seriously for a moment?"

"Sure, I guess."

"Well— "

"Cat got your tongue? I haven't known you long, but I've never known you to be at a loss for words," he prodded.

"Okay, Michael, here's the thing. I am concerned about your drinking."

"What? The bars are where we have most of our fun," Michael pushed back.

"I know that, but your alcohol abuse is getting out of hand."

"Can't a guy drink a little without people getting on his case? It's not like I'm some knock-down, fall-down drunk," Michael grumbled.

"Are you sure about that? You're drunk all the time. I've seen you get behind the wheel of a car after hours of heavy drinking. You could get hurt or, worse, killed."

"That's a load of crap. I have it under control. Nothing to worry about."

"Listen to yourself. You're in denial. The people you are hanging around are not a good influence. They are not your friends. Friends should be honest with you. They wouldn't encourage you to buy rounds for everyone. Wake up. These guys are dragging you down."

"I don't have to listen to this. We hardly know each other. What gives you the right?"

"I have feelings for you. You need help."

"I don't need anyone's help or . . . pity."

"This isn't pity. It's a gesture of friendship. May I ask you to do one thing for me?"

"What's that?"

"Come with me to my church. Listen to the pastor's sermon."

"I don't know. I'm not very religious."

"We can leave if you don't like it."

"I won't like it."

"Will you try it once? For me?"

Michael finally agreed to attend a single service after it became clear that Sarah would not take no for an answer. He tried to listen and absorb the pastor's words but was distracted.

He walked out of the service and into the nearest tavern. Sarah followed him, desperately trying to restrict his drinking. When she asked for his keys, he stormed out of the bar, hopped into the Jag, and took off.

The Detroit Police later pulled him over on I-75. They clocked him on radar doing over one hundred miles per hour in a sixty-five-mile zone. The cops performed field sobriety and breathalyzer tests. Michael blew almost double the legal limit. The officers arrested him for speeding, reckless driving, and driving under the influence. They transported him to the Wayne County Jail and tossed him into the drunk tank.

"Hello?"

"Is this Stanley O'Hara?"

"Yes."

"We have your son down at Wayne County. He asked us to call you. He needs a lawyer."

"What did he do?"

"Speeding. Drunk and reckless driving, sir. He blew point nineteen."

"Shit! I'll be right there."

Call it a force of habit, but after rescuing his son from the drunk tank, Stanley O'Hara used his considerable political influence to make the charges go away. He retained the finest criminal lawyer in the county, who negotiated a plea, suspended sentence, and record expungement. For his part, Michael surrendered his license, promised to attend AA meetings, and entered a driver education program. He felt ashamed but grateful that he didn't hurt or kill anyone.

In addition to meeting all the requirements of his plea agreement, Michael reconnected with Sarah. They began to attend church services. After several sermons, Michael began to reconsider his post-Taggert life. He confessed his deep feelings of betrayal and self-doubt. Sarah encouraged him to counsel with the pastor, where Michael acknowledged he inflicted pain upon himself and others. The pastor brought him to tears and urged him to rediscover his better self.

Michael opened his soul and expressed feelings to Sarah in ways he never experienced. He learned that no man is defined by his worst moments in life. He could choose to be defined by life's finest moments.

As a lawyer who once did *pro bono* work, he realized how misguided he was about power and financial success. He was corrupted into thinking that winning and money were everything. Sarah and her pastor helped him understand the meaning of *Tikkun Olam* from the Hebrew bible. His new mission in life was to take responsibility for his actions, heal, improve, and perfect the world around him.

Michael O'Hara now felt better about things. Could he put his past behind him and move on? Sarah wasn't sure, but she took pride in his transformation, his *metamorphosis*, as she referred to it. At the same time, she fell madly in love with him.

However, there was one aspect of his previous life's skin that Michael could not shed. He enjoyed being with Sarah but could not stop thinking about another woman. He couldn't shake her or understand why. They shared a couple of meals and tried a case together. What was this *hold* she had on him? *I'm capable of multiple relationships at the same time. I can chew gum and walk.*

One night, Michael and Sarah met for dinner at *Lelli's*, a well-known Italian eatery where Michael commanded a corner table. Until that moment, their time together had been spent in bars or church.

Sarah believed the evening would be dedicated to furthering their relationship. Would he ask her to move in with him? Would he go full Monty, get on his knees, and ask her to marry him?

Instead, he stunned her and said: "Sarah. Thanks for everything. I'm a better person for having known you. We can't see each other any longer."

"What? I *love* you. I'm *in love* with you. We've been to hell and back together. I knew you didn't share my feelings, but I thought you *cared* for me, at the very least, that we were hitting it off, heading for a meaningful relationship." She grabbed the napkin from her lap and dabbed the tears that overwhelmed her eyes.

"I *do* care for you, Sarah. That's why I'm doing this. I'd only make you miserable." He reached for her hand. She jerked it away.

"After all we've been through, I can't believe you would throw away a chance at true love," she sputtered.

Frustrated and angry, she picked up her full glass of water, threw it in his face, and stormed out of the restaurant. Initially, Michael was stunned and embarrassed. Upon reflection, he didn't blame her. *I deserved it.* Michael took his napkin and wiped his face. His shirt was soaking wet.

The server came over and asked if there was anything he could do. He offered Michael a free restaurant tee shirt. Michael took him up on the offer but insisted that he add the shirt to the bill. The waiter brought the shirt. Michael entered the bathroom, changed clothes, and returned to pay the bill. Patrons glared and snickered at him in his new shirt. He looked like a restaurant server or busboy. They mocked him to their companions and enjoyed a laugh at his expense.

Michael didn't care. He did the right thing by Sarah. He realigned his thoughts and heard words through a new filter. He exited the restaurant and scanned the area, looking for Sarah. She was long gone, probably on her way home in a taxi or Uber. He felt terrible but knew her pain would be worse if he strung her along. He hoped, with time, she'd realize that simple truth. Perhaps they could one day be friends.

He texted for an Uber. The driver arrived, and Michael climbed into the back seat on the passenger side. As the driver drove off into the night, Michael's thoughts drifted from Sarah to Taggert, Longbow, and finally, to Andrea.

Her strength of purpose and commitment to her client were dynamic and impressive. Those qualities won her the case; *those and a ton of evidence!* He laughed out loud. The driver studied him in the rearview mirror. Michael still had difficulty accepting the loss. *Was Andrea a better lawyer? Or did she have a better case?*

In the days and weeks that followed, Michael worked on his sobriety. He hoped to resume his practice and needed his driver's license. He hung out at diners with his AA buddies, people who punched a clock for a living. The experience helped him appreciate privilege's distinct advantages, being born to wealthy, influential, and politically connected people. His friends jokingly called him a member of the lucky sperm club.

He shot pool with these men, played ping pong, foosball, talked politics, and watched football. He listened to their troubles and stories about their spouses and children. He answered legal questions. He discovered they had much in common. Each wanted a happy domestic life, marriage, children, and a steady job. Michael wanted to return to the practice of law. As he pondered his future, his thoughts kept returning to Andrea Kramer.

"What is it?" He asked himself aloud. *Is it that she beat me in court in the most significant case of my career?* He couldn't understand his feelings. *Do I crave a rematch? What's the allure?*

Suddenly, it hit him. Andrea was the real deal. She had no airs about her. She was authentic, genuine, and loyal. She had her client's back. *That's* why she worked so hard. *That's* why she had his loyalty. He wanted *that.* He determined to get to know Andrea Kramer. *But how?*

They were from two different worlds. Michael only knew privileged life, with shallow country club types, silk-stocking lawyers, stock portfolios, and two martini lunches. *How, indeed!*

CHAPTER FOURTEEN

Andrea

"Why not? I fell at the Secretary of State's office. The floor was wet. It's a good case. I'm suffering!" A prospective client argued. "Sue the state. It's your specialty, isn't it?"

"Mr. Peterson, we did a preliminary investigation. The Secretary of State has cameras. Let's agree that the accident didn't happen as you said. According to the adjuster, you have filed sixteen slip and fall claims in the last three years."

Andrea was careful not to use the word 'fraud.' She didn't want to disparage the man.

"These state offices don't keep their floors clean. They don't care about us citizens. It was not my fault."

"I must be truthful with you here, sir. You don't have a case. You think the state will pay, but Michigan law does not support your claim. There was no moisture on your clothing. Witnesses say the floor was dry. It had not rained in a few days. They have the whole thing on video. Do you understand what I'm telling you? You do not want to pursue this. My suggestion to you is to learn from this and move forward."

"Aren't lawyers supposed to give their clients the benefit of the doubt? You must take my case," Peterson demanded.

"I'm not obligated to do anything, sir. I can't take a case I don't believe in. In this case, I *did* give you the benefit of the doubt. I filed the claim and investigated the circumstances. You won't prevail under Michigan law."

"The newspapers say you help the little guy in court. You sued the state and won lots of money. I read all about it. Why can't you do the same for me?"

"Mr. Longbow had a legitimate claim. You do not. We both understand what you're trying to do. There might be a lawyer out there who would try to get you compensation. I'm not one of them. I'll send you a termination letter in the mail. Good luck to you."

Andrea pushed her chair back, stood, and extended her hand over the desktop. Their eyes met as she closed the meeting with body language that ordered him to leave. Peterson stood, shrugged, shook her hand, and left the office.

Phony claims were a miserable side effect of having a busy law office. Peterson was a poor scam artist. The Longbow case changed everything for Andrea. Her office phone was ringing off the hook. She received hundreds of emails weekly, begging for her assistance.

"You can afford to be choosy," Sheila advised by telephone. "Embrace your new-found fame. Take full advantage, but make sure the cases you accept are worthy of an attorney of your caliber. You have become O'Hara on steroids. I'll bet he wishes he were you these days."

"I doubt it. I haven't heard from him recently, especially since the Taggert firm let him go. I feel responsible in some way. He probably feels the same. I'm sure he's got a pile of money stashed somewhere. He'll land on his feet."

"If you say so."

"I know so."

The bell at the front door jingled. Andrea could not see the visitor from her office. She leaned forward, put her hand over the receiver, and called out.

"Have a seat. I'll be right with you."

"New client?" Sheila asked on the other side of the line.

"I'm not sure. The girls are at lunch. I didn't think I had any more appointments today." Andrea flipped through her iPad schedule. "Hang on. I'd better go see—"

As she peeked out and saw the visitor, the telephone was suddenly yanked from her hand. It fell to the ground with a thud. Andrea heard Sheila's distant voice over the receiver.

"Andrea? Are you alright? Andi?"

Andrea scrambled to retrieve her phone from the floor.

"Yes . . . I'm fine . . . I've got to go, Sheila. Michael O'Hara is standing in my office."

"Whoa! Is that karma, or is that karma? What are you going to do? Andi?"

Andrea disconnected the call. "Michael! What a pleasant surprise! Did we have an appointment?" she rambled.

"No, we didn't. Nothing like that. I was in the neighborhood." He sniffed the air. "What's that smell?"

"What smell?" Her heart skipped a beat. She could feel it pounding in her chest at the mere sight of him. She recalled his body language—he stood that way whenever he decided to be charming. His dazzling smile disarmed her. There he was, all six-foot-four of him, within an arm's length, and Andrea had no idea why.

"What are you doing here?"

"Do you have time for coffee?"

"My staff is at lunch . . . no one to watch the office—" Andrea couldn't catch her breath. She felt like Ingrid Bergman when she first saw Bogie in *Casablanca*. "W-what is it you w-want to t-talk about?"

"I have a proposition," he declared.

Andrea held her breath. She exhaled audibly. Embarrassed, she looked away. *I'm behaving like a schoolgirl.*

"What kind of proposition?"

"Coffee?"

"Why not?" She finally decided. "I'll lock the office and turn on the answering service. I doubt anything earth-shattering will happen."

She closed the office. He sniffed, his nose wrinkling. *Does he smell something?* He did a three-sixty, checking out the office décor. *What did he expect?* The place was still a work in progress.

"How about that place over there?" He stared out the front window and took her elbow. A warm tingle shot through her body. Michael pointed her arm at *Dunfee's*, a bit high-class for Saline workers but a popular spot for a coffee klatch of ladies.

"That'll work," she agreed. "It's more your style than *Maggie's* or *The Meltdown.*"

A short walk from the office, the coffee shop had a cozy, homey atmosphere, warm lighting, and mismatched furniture. The walls were decorated with vintage framed art, giving the cafe a unique, eclectic feel. The wooden floor was stained a warm brown and covered with colorful rugs. The place had several small tables with comfortable chairs, perfect for coffee, a light snack, and casual banter.

The counter had freshly baked pastries, cakes, and other treats. The baristas were friendly and knowledgeable and made a perfect cup. The smell of freshly brewed coffee and warm pastries filled the air, creating a relaxing atmosphere.

Michael cut a dashing figure as he walked into the cafe. Women turned and glared at the couple. Michael's tall frame, broad shoulders, and confident posture gave him an air of sophistication.

"Nice place," he murmured.

He walked to a table by the window and held out a chair. Andrea dutifully followed and sat in the chair. The warm, welcoming atmosphere of the cafe seemed to humble him. His usually meticulously styled black hair was tousled, framing his striking blue eyes. Andrea's breath caught in her throat. She stared at him. He was the picture of perfection, and she couldn't help smiling.

"Why are you smiling? Something on my face?" He rubbed at his mouth and chin.

"Nothing like that." She shook her head and blushed.

"What, then?"

"Nothing. You look . . . perfect."

He laughed—music to her ears.

"Perfect? I thought you hated my guts."

"That's not true. I never *hated* you," she began. "I didn't care for your cocksure, arrogant attitude during discovery and trial."

"I adopt that persona to intimidate my opponents. It did not intimidate you. You kicked my ass."

"As I told you back then, I had the better case." She glanced down, nervous. When she looked up, he stared at her with a slight smile. She shook her head again slowly, her blush deepening.

"What?"

"Nothing. It's nothing . . . You . . . I . . . You look *amazing*."

They sat at the table, lost in each other's gaze.

"What can I get you?" A server interrupted, breaking their trance. Michael ordered coffee for two and a coffee roll to share. The server left the table.

"So . . . how the hell are you? Enjoying your new-found fame?" Michael smiled.

She laughed. His carefree banter was so much better than the sarcastic, acidic tone he'd adopted during the trial.

"Doing well," she replied. "Busy as hell. Achieve some fame, and prospective clients come crawling out of the woodwork. You do have to watch for the cockroaches, though."

Michael laughed. The server returned with their coffee and coffee roll.

Andrea sipped the coffee. "How about you?" she asked. "How the hell are *you*?"

He shrugged. "*Better* is the best way I can answer. As you probably know, I've had a tough time since the verdict. Things have been rocky, but they're improving. I guess you could call me a work in progress. I'm trying to figure out what to do with the rest of my life."

She nodded. "I heard Taggert let you go. That's tough. You did nothing to deserve that. I'm sorry. But you're here, still upright. You look great. I'm sure you'll figure things out."

He smiled and took a sip of his coffee. His eyes stared deep into her soul. She became woozy. *Where is this conversation heading?*

"Thanks. I sure hope so."

They continued to catch up and engage in light banter. Michael told her about his post-Taggert professional endeavors and his casual search for employment. Usually so confident, she enjoyed this candid, somewhat unsure version of Michael O'Hara.

"I'm not entirely telling you the truth," he admitted.

She raised an eyebrow. "Oh? What is the entire truth?"

He took a deep breath. "I've decided to open an office and start a solo practice."

Her eyes widened with surprise. She smiled. "That's great! I'm sure you will be a huge success."

"Thanks, Andrea. That means a lot to me."

"Where's the new office? Detroit? Downtown? Troy, Southfield?" She pictured a deluxe high-rise building. There were plenty to choose from.

"No," he shook his head. "I'm going to try a small-town practice. I'm going to do it here." He looked around the coffee shop as if he planned to practice from a table in the corner.

"What?" She blanched. "You mean, here in Saline?"

He nodded, a slight smirk on his face. "Yep. Right here in Saline. I figure small-town folks might enjoy talking to a big-city lawyer. I plan to bring the big city to the small town. What do you think?"

Andrea chuckled. "That's the dumbest thing I've ever heard. It's a ridiculous idea. Small-town people move to Saline to escape the city and big-town people. Get it? People are different here, Michael."

Michael nodded and laughed. "True. I remember the shit-shoes man," he groaned and gagged. Andrea laughed.

"Seriously, though, I plan to be the exception. People are just going to have to get used to me. I'm looking forward to it. Please? Be happy for me," Michael implored.

Andrea *was* excited. This was a significant change for Michael. She admired his courage. However, she was ambivalent about him being that close to her all the time. *How do I feel?* She reached across the table, grabbed his hand, and felt his pulse.

"Your pulse is strong. You look good and seem healthy enough. Have you gone mad?" They laughed.

"Maybe a little," he grinned. He was serious about the practice. "But that's what I am going to do. I mean . . . I'm doing it."

Andrea shook her head. "I can see you're serious. I see it in your eyes. But you can't open a practice here. You just can't!"

"Why not?"

"Because it's ridiculous, that's all. It's a crazy idea. Seriously? For one thing, Saline doesn't need you."

"Not true from what I can see."

"From what you . . . wait just a minute, buster." Her eyes flashed to her office, down the street. "How long have you been watching my office? Who do you think you are? CIA?"

"The CIA only spies out of the country. Domestically, I would be FBI."

"Funny. You're a load of laughs," she bristled.

"To answer your question, though, I've been here for a few days. I needed to get the lay of the land, so to speak." He shot her that smile that made her heart stop.

"Your office is visible from my hotel room. I sat in the room for a day and a half trying to figure out the right way to tell you. I started to feel like a stalker . . . no . . . a *voyeur.* I finally decided to walk over and give you the news straight from the horse's mouth."

"Great, Michael, open your practice. Just not in Saline. How about Ann Arbor? That's close by. Or the west side of the state, Benton Harbor, St. Joe, or Muskegon? Better yet, how about California? The women will love you!"

"Nah." He taunted her now, shaking his head. "I like it here. It's close to family. A good place to start for someone who has a lot to learn. And I have a lot to learn about running a law practice."

Andrea glared at him. *I hate this, don't I?* Or perhaps she liked the idea a little bit. She was confused about her feelings. She struggled to find more reasons to talk him out of this madness. Strands of reddish-brown hair fell over her forehead and across her face. She gazed at him and was surprised and touched when he reached out and gently tucked strands behind her ear.

"Thank you," she whispered.

He smiled. "Anytime."

Out of words, they stared at each other, stretching out the moment until the server brought more coffee. They spent the rest of their time together, talking, laughing, and enjoying each other's company. Michael was too good to be true, Andrea decided. *But is he right for Saline?*

CHAPTER FIFTEEN

Michael

Michael enjoyed his coffee date with Andrea. The date bolstered his resolve to be near her, to establish his law practice in Saline. All he needed was a central location.

Unlike Andrea, money was no object, yet it was. He couldn't swoop into Andrea's town and open the type of office he was used to. He could afford it, sure, but he would make her look small and insignificant by comparison. He refused to do anything to hurt her.

He contacted a realtor and told her what he wanted. She showed him every workable space in town. Some spaces were close, but he refused to settle. The agent put him in touch with a build-to-suit unit. He toyed with building his dream office. He nixed the idea when the owner said construction would take months rather than weeks. He began to reconsider his plans.

Maybe he'd take Andrea's advice and open his office in nearby Ann Arbor. *The best of both worlds*, he rationalized. The University of Michigan made Ann Arbor a small town with a big-town feel. Maybe he'd return to his roots—open an office in the same building as the Taggert firm, compete with them, take their corporate and government clients, and put those pricks out of business. He smiled at the thought.

But he knew it wasn't realistic. He was running out of options. He stood outside his motel room and gazed at the central business district. His eyes focused on the old house and barn, and he suddenly realized the solution to his problem. *I'm such an idiot. It's been staring at me the whole time!*

"Hello again." He tapped on the frame of her doorway. She was preoccupied with a file but glanced up, surprised, just as he had hoped.

"You wouldn't have any office space for rent, would you?" He was unabashed, as usual, cocky almost, like he was doing her a favor. His tone, though, was friendly.

"This isn't your style, Michael. Why would you want to rent here?" Andrea was perplexed.

"I don't know. I hear the landlord is a terrific person."

"Very funny." She feigned a return to work, picked up a file folder, and opened it. She pretended to write something on the back of an envelope but only scribbled.

"Breaking in a new pen, are we?" He noted her scribbles.

"We? Do you think I'm that easy?"

"I don't know. Are you?" He wiggled his eyebrows. Did his best impression of Groucho Marx. The double entendre was unmistakable.

Andrea dropped the file again and fell back in her chair. A resigned sigh escaped her lips. "Michael, what do you want from me?" she grumbled.

He had a glib response ready for her but decided to keep things real.

"The truth?" He stepped forward, flipped the chair opposite her, and sat down with the back of the chair in front of him.

"Interesting," she observed.

"Interesting, what? What's interesting?"

"The way you flipped the chair. You're a control freak. This is *my* office. That is *my* chair. The chair was fine where it was, turned the correct way, yet you had to flip it, adjust it to your whim."

"What the . . . are you some sort of psychologist?"

She picked up her pen and twiddled it between her fingers like a baton. "I don't need to be a psychologist to understand basic human body language. Didn't they teach you that in law school?"

"I must have missed that class."

"That's a shame. It might have made a difference for you," a not-so-subtle reference to her trial victory.

Michael winced. Andrea felt instantly guilty.

"Cheap shot. Sorry."

He ignored the apology. "Now, about your question. What do I want from you? I want a first-floor office—I don't like heights. I want to try a small-town practice, perhaps build something from scratch. I admire you. I want to get to know you better. You've got space. I need space. We're a match made in heaven," he chirped with a disarming smile.

She hesitated and looked him in the eye before answering.

"A match made in heaven, huh? I'm not a fan of bullshit—are you playing games with me? What do you *want,* Michael?"

"I want what you have. A small-town office where I can start my practice. If I'm being sincere, I want to be closer, perhaps explore the possibility of us."

"Us?" She didn't dismiss the idea.

"Yes, us, the beginnings of a relationship. Uh . . . a business relationship," he clarified. "You have more space than you need. I need a place in Saline to hang my shingle. I'm a good lawyer. You said so yourself. I can help with the overflow. See? Made in heaven." He pointed to the sky.

"Come on. Get real. We come from two different sides of the track. Two different *worlds*. You're going to open an office in my haunted house? Isn't this beneath the O'Hara pedigree? You could open a law office *anywhere*. Why *here*? This won't work."

He leaned forward, his eyes earnest. "You taught me some important lessons during our time together."

"I'm glad . . . I think," she chuckled, leaning back in her office chair.

Michael stood and began to pace. He turned back to her, started to say something, and stopped. He resumed pacing. She waited patiently. Finally, he turned to her a second time.

"I know we come from different backgrounds. I'm sure people from all walks of life come into this place looking for legal assistance. Different backgrounds and lifestyles might be a positive. Ever think of that? I understand you're not on board yet, but I promise to do my best to fit in here. I'm serious," he argued.

Andrea paused for a moment before speaking. She gradually met Michael's gaze.

"You have zero understanding of small-town life. There will be a tremendous learning curve."

"I'm willing to learn."

He had an answer for everything. Andrea felt herself relenting. "What about the smell?"

"I'll get used to it. What *is* that, by the way?"

"They say that people *died* in here."

"So . . . what? Their bodies are still around?"

"That's the legend."

"I'll get used to it," he promised. He shot her a desperate look, the coup de grâce. How could she refuse that face?

"Okay, Michael. Against my better judgment—"

"Thank you! I love you!" He jumped out of his chair.

"You *love* me? I'm rethinking this already."

"Funny, Kramer. You know what I mean."

"Yes, I do. Welcome to Kramer Law." A chill ran down her spine. She wasn't sure about his intentions but was willing to give his plan a trial period.

Michael paced the floor. "I've got to order some furniture and supplies. Is there anything you need?"

"I'm good. See you tomorrow?"

"Bright and early, boss."

"Don't call me boss."

***

Michael enjoyed the shocked look on Andrea's face when she arrived at the office the following morning. There he sat, waiting on her front porch.

"How long have you been sitting here?"

"I don't know. A half-hour, maybe. You forgot to give me a key."

"I don't have a spare key. We'll have to get one made."

He carried a briefcase and a laptop. A stack of small boxes sat to the left of the door. Andrea pulled out a key and unlocked the door, holding it open for him. He kicked a crate with his leg and wedged it into the opening so the door would not close.

"Where to, my lady?" He smiled.

"Good morning to you, too," she smiled back. "Follow me."

Michael was eager to get started but sensed that Andrea continued to have reservations about taking him on. He could tell, for instance, that his early arrival this morning was unexpected. As she showed him around the place, she still appeared conflicted. They were venturing into unknown territory.

"What's wrong?" Michael asked, reading the signs of distress.

Andrea took a deep breath and let it out slowly. "I'm just nervous," she replied, looking away. "This is new and different for both of us. Are we ready? I wish I had a crystal ball."

"Everything will be fine. We need to set boundaries and respect them. I *have* a crystal ball that says that going into business with Andrea Kramer is a wonderful idea."

She laughed. "I must confess, your faith in this endeavor is contagious."

"Glad to hear it," he cheered.

"Here's your office, counselor. That aftershave you wear should cover the smell."

They stood in the back of the building in front of a carved-out fourteen-by-fourteen space. It had three sides and no door.

"I'm not sure why it's open like that," Andrea said. "When we start making money, we'll build out the front and add a door. At least it's quiet and semi-private back here."

Michael chuckled and surveyed the room. He turned to Andrea with a grin on his face.

"It's perfect," he declared, touching her shoulder.

"You really like it? It's a far cry from Taggert, Miles, & Freeman and the 36th floor."

"What's not to like? As I said before, it's perfect. I love it. Besides, *you're* here."

He stepped closer and studied her eyes. "I've followed your interviews, public appearances, and advocacy since the Longbow verdict. You're doing amazing things here. I'm honored you've invited me to be part of it."

"I didn't exactly invite you. You showed up at my front door after stalking me for two days, remember?"

"Indeed, I do, and I am forever grateful to you for getting this homeless lawyer off the streets. I won't let you down." He gave her shoulder a warm squeeze.

Michael went to work. He located two carts in a storeroom at the back of the building, wheeled them toward a corner in his new office, and positioned them side-by-side. He found an old countertop, perhaps from what was once the kitchen, and laid it across the carts, creating a makeshift desk. He then secured each end with thick clamps.

Michael unpacked his laptop and document folders, neatly arranging them on the countertop. He placed his sleek leather briefcase full of legal documents on the bottom of the carts, within easy reach. A workable office materialized out of spare parts, its handiwork gleaming with a smidgeon of the O'Hara pride and cockiness Andrea despised during the trial. An old executive chair he found in a storage room completed his masterpiece.

Michael stepped back for one final inspection, smiled with satisfaction, and sat behind the desk. It was official. His law office was open for business. Pulling his laptop closer, he ran his fingers across the smooth metal exterior and opened the cover. A peck on several keys, and the machine came to life. He took an inspired deep breath.

Despite challenging conditions that forced him to try this new and unusual business model away from Detroit, he felt energized to begin this journey. He pledged to make the most of the opportunity. Andrea walked into the office and looked around.

"Not bad, O'Hara, not bad. Talk about making something out of nothing. Where did you find this stuff? What made you think of using old carts and a countertop to make a desk?"

"There are all kinds of useful spare parts lying around this place. I went on a scavenger hunt. Pretty cool, huh?"

"Yes, I'm impressed. What about a phone?" Andrea asked. "My phone system should accommodate an extra line or two. My receptionist can answer your phone."

Michael held up his cell phone. "I'll use this for now—take you up on the offer, though. I'll need at least two lines for a main hub. After all, I plan to stick around a while."

"I'll talk to the equipment people and find out what's what."

"Thanks, Andrea, I appreciate it. And I will pay my fair share for the phone lines and the use of the receptionist."

"I'm excited. I've got plenty of overflow work because of my sudden notoriety from the Longbow verdict. You're a talented trial lawyer. I hope to take full advantage of you."

"I'm excited as well, for the opposite reason. The Longbow verdict has me needing a fresh start."

Embarking on a new business took work, but Michael would be successful if determination and confidence translated into success. He seemed ready to tackle whatever came his way. The office decor was a makeshift solution, but it would do for now. His dream became a reality as he gathered the necessary items for his business venture.

"At some point, as we grow together, we'll refurbish the place. My treat! I'll hire some contractors, give it a facelift, buy office furniture, and hire staff. We can swap these costs for rent. What do you think?" Michael asked.

"I appreciate the gesture, but it's a bit premature, wouldn't you say?"

Michael shook his head and took one of her hands. "Don't worry. I'm not doing anything right away. Whatever I do, it will be an investment in our mutual success. We're going to turn this place into a source of pride. Make it the talk of the town."

"So long as we do it together, I'm on board," Andrea smiled. "I'm not a charity case. We've got lots of new business coming in, and the appeals on Longbow are almost exhausted."

"Understood and acknowledged. The trial was clean. You'll win the appeal," Michael assured her.

"If that's the case, I don't need to tell you about the contingency fee. I'll be able to more than pay my fair share. Together, or not at all," she insisted.

"Deal." They shook on it. Michael took her in his arms and hugged her. The gesture came naturally to him. He sat, swiveled his chair, reached down, and returned to face Andrea. He held a bottle of Vernor's Ginger Ale and two champagne glasses.

"A toast to our new endeavor," he chirped.

"Vernor's?"

"I've stopped drinking. It's all part of my master plan. Besides, Vernor's is a Detroit legend. There's an elementary school named after the founder."

"By all means then," she agreed. "A Vernor's toast your fancy new office."

Michael laughed and twisted the cap. Pop shot out and hit him in the face. Pop and foam dribbled down Michael's face and chin. His shirt was soaked.

"Shit!" He scowled.

Andrea stared, wide-eyed, mouth open. She paused and broke into hysterical laughter.

"What's so funny? Vernor's is fizzy. Shit happens. Don't just stand there laughing. Towel, please? What kind of landlord are you?"

Andrea stayed put, cracking up. After a pregnant pause, Michael started to laugh. Soon, they were both in hysterics. Andrea left to retrieve a towel. When she returned, Michael was shirtless. Andrea handed him the towel and stared. Michael noticed her reaction, pleased she was enjoying the view. She'd never seen him shirtless. Michael dried himself.

"The last time this happened was at *Lelli's*," Michael cracked. He knew Andrea had no idea what he was talking about.

Sufficiently dry, Michael poured some pop and handed a glass to Andrea. He held his glass in the air.

"To the Haunted Barn Law Office. May we enjoy nothing but success, personally and professionally."

Andrea giggled. Michael was pleased with her reaction.

"Here, here! That name has a certain ring to it." Andrea held up her glass. "To our success."

"Any old shirts lying around this place?"

The Haunted Barn Law Office was unofficially born at that moment. To the public, it was 'The Andrea Kramer Law Firm,' owned and operated by its famous proprietor. Michael O'Hara, well-known only in Detroit, would have to *earn* his legal chops in small-town USA.

CHAPTER SIXTEEN

Michael

Over the next few weeks, Michael worked diligently, coordinating workers and work schedules, assembling furniture, securing supplies and equipment, and otherwise making things happen. The two lawyers agreed on most things, but when they didn't, Andrea commented on Michael's ability to compromise, find workable solutions, and get results, no matter how challenging the situation.

"You'd make a terrific mediator," Andrea praised.

Michael's expertise and work ethic helped the practice grow. Business was booming. People from all over the area somehow found their way to the Kramer Law Offices, seeking legal advice and representation. Michael became integral to the process, especially the business end of things, which permitted Andrea to handle the more complicated and challenging tort cases. With Michael's management guidance, everyone's hard work, and a little luck along the way, it seemed that nothing could derail the enormous growth of the business.

That's when Vincent Smith walked into the office. Michael greeted him and led him to the conference room. He buzzed Andrea and asked her to join him.

"Welcome, Mr. Smith. What can we do for you today?"

"I own a toy company, Smith Toys. We had to recall a line of toy soldiers because of some claims that the soldiers presented a choke hazard. We're being sued. Frankly, we've done extensive research and other due diligence, tested the product up the wazoo, and we've concluded that this is a money grab. Plaintiffs' attorneys are attempting to stick it to the military and the gun industry and found a deep-pocket defendant to be their patsy."

Michael glanced at Andrea. This differed from the type of case she had in mind for their collaboration. For Michael, a corporate and insurance *defense* lawyer, it sounded like a jackpot case.

"I wouldn't be surprised if they tried to turn this into a multi-district case. This is right in my wheelhouse. I'm sure I can limit the damage," Michael assured. "This anti-military sentiment is the very definition of *woke*. American parents and children need to toughen up."

"Michael, can we talk, please?" Andrea interrupted.

"Hang on a second, Andrea. This is important." He held up a finger and continued. "I've got a corporate pedigree. I've represented government entities, large and small corporations, and insurance companies."

"I'm aware. I did my research on you. You got a raw deal on that insurrection case," Smith advised.

"Thanks for saying that. I completely agree." They laughed. Andrea did not.

"Michael, I insist we talk," Andrea persisted. She rose and pointed to the door.

"Will you excuse me for a moment, Mr. Smith? This can't wait. He glared at Andrea and rolled his eyes. They left the conference room. Michael followed Andrea to her office. When they got there, she unloaded.

"What the hell, Michael?"

"What the hell, what, Andrea?" They weren't communicating.

"Smith toys? A dangerous choke hazard masked as a toy? This is the opposite of what my firm is about."

"Whoa, Andrea! Hold the phone! We don't *know* if these toys are choke hazards or dangerous in any way. We only know the company has been sued."

"We'd be doing Mr. Smith and his company a disservice if we didn't do careful research before declaring war against so-called woke parents. Don't you think? I could never represent a company whose product chokes children," Andrea argued.

"I agree research is necessary, but let's get something straight. You won't represent Smith Toys. I will," Michael retorted.

"But I thought we were building a practice together," she challenged.

"We are. We will. But we're not yet where we hope to be. Am I a member of your firm? Are you paying me? Or am I a tenant?"

"You're a tenant, but I thought that was a first step. You know, baby steps, remember? Get to know each other and all that."

"Right, and while we get to know each other, I've got to make a living. This guy is my dream client. Taggert would have given me a huge bonus if I brought in a client like this," Michael contended.

"So, refer it to Taggert."

"You're joking. We are talking six, maybe even seven-figure fees here. I'm not letting this guy out the door." Michael folded his arms.

"What if Smith Toy victims want to retain me? If the toys are defective, I will see some cases, and we'll be on opposite sides. You don't see a conflict of interest?"

"No. We operate out of the same building. We are not the same law firm. Clients are free to retain you. Besides, isn't this cart before horse? Right now, you don't have a single client who wants to sue Smith Toys." Michael doubled down. This case and the client were too enticing. Huge corporate fees flooded his mind.

Andrea

Andrea was wounded. She thought the idea was to practice *together*. At the first opportunity to generate corporate fees, Michael sought a separation. She expressed her disappointment, but he couldn't pass on what he called a "fabulous opportunity." The two lawyers returned to the conference room and Mr. Smith.

Andrea spoke first. "I'm going to step away, Mr. Smith. Michael wishes to represent you. Work out those details with him. We have an office-sharing arrangement. I am a civil trial lawyer and may represent Smith Toy victims in the future. If a Smith Toy victim retains me, I am confident Michael and I can create the proper separation and division of personnel. I will excuse myself now and let you two finish your business. Good luck to you, Mr. Smith. You have a terrific lawyer. Thanks for coming in," Andrea concluded.

"That works for me," Smith replied. "Thanks for your sincerity and for walking me through the process, Ms. Kramer. I can see why the citizens love working with you. Michael is a great fit for my situation."

Andrea left Michael's office. A half-hour later, Smith and O'Hara walked into the vestibule and shook hands. Andrea watched out her window as Smith entered his Porsche SUV, backed away from the building, and drove off.

Shortly afterward, there was a knock on her door.

"Come in."

Michael opened the door and peeked his head into the office.

"May I come in? Are you mad at me? Truce?"

"I'm not mad at you. We have different concepts and expectations for our business relationship. Consider the relationship clarified."

"Don't be like that. You've never represented a client like Smith. How can I pass on hundreds of thousands, perhaps millions, in repeat corporate fees? It's what I do, what I'm *good* at."

"As I said, I'm sorry I misunderstood. I won't stand in your way. But that goes both ways. You can't play both sides. Good luck with your new client. I'm busy if there is nothing else." She looked past him to the lobby.

"What is your problem?" Michael grumbled.

"No problem," she huffed. "I have work to do."

"Come on, Andrea. We need to talk this out. There were bound to be issues, case crossovers, and the like. We have different practice interests. We'll do better with separate clients. Less redundancy, don't you think?"

"My firm does not represent corporate interests that have wronged Michigan citizens. I thought you understood that. We can never work cases together while you represent evil Goliaths like Smith. We will forever be on opposite sides."

"Opposites attract, don't you think?" he kibbitzed. She scowled and remained silent.

"Corporations aren't necessarily evil in litigation. Plaintiffs aren't always innocent victims," Michael continued.

Andrea nodded in agreement. "You're correct, of course. I just dumped a guy this morning. He filed sixteen premises cases in two years. But I could never do what you do: represent the government against a guy like Longbow. I thought you were through with that life. What if Smith's toys are hazardous?"

"Then he'll have to pay to fix the problem. He's going to find representation somewhere. Why not here? As we move forward, how about we agree to focus on what we both bring to the table? Try to find clients that best fit each of our skill sets. No conflicts, no one covers the same ground."

"That's fine, but we will never work *together.* You get that, right?"

"I couldn't let six-to-seven-figure fees walk out the door. We'll figure this out over time." He quietly backed out of her office and returned to his own.

Michael stayed quiet and away from Andrea for the rest of the afternoon. At closing time, he poked his head into her office.

"Grab a bite to eat?"

Andrea hesitated for a moment before answering. "I'm not sure that's a good idea," she decided, gazing at the floor. "We've got a lot of thinking to do. This stuff is better discussed after a good night's sleep."

She forced herself to meet his eyes and offered a small smile. "After we hash all this out, okay?"

Michael scowled and shrugged his shoulders, obviously disappointed with Andrea's take on the Smith Toys litigation. Still, he nodded in agreement. "Okay," he finally responded. "Have a great evening."

He turned and left the building. After he was gone, Andrea sighed. *How do I feel?*

One moment, she hoped for a successful business and, perhaps, a personal relationship. *The next moment, he's working for the dark side.* While they could still make things work, clients like Vincent Smith made things difficult. Could they at least co-exist? She hoped they could be professional about the situation.

Their meeting the following morning was more of the same—it did not go well. Andrea wanted Michael to be more than a suitemate. She wanted a partner. Formal arrangement in writing or not, she wanted to work with a like-minded attorney, someone who shared her vision of helping those who needed the most help.

Michael expressed his desire for freedom. He wanted to choose his cases and clients.

"I can't pass up business I've handled my whole career. Especially with the fees these cases will generate."

The two were at an impasse. They decided to continue to share space. Michael would hang his shingle, separate and distinct from Andrea's practice. They would keep two sets of books and records, create separate corporate entities, and share employees and office expenses. The employees might work with both attorneys occasionally but could not share confidential client information.

Publicly, Andrea sincerely hoped it would be a workable relationship. Privately, she had doubts. Worse, she had developed *feelings* for Michael. Being on opposite sides in business made a personal relationship difficult.

Andrea noted one important commonality. Both lawyers worked hard, leaving little time to discuss business or pleasure. On top of their work schedules, workers were constantly in and out of the office, disrupting things, shutting off power, making lots of noise, and getting in everyone's way. Michael called it short-term pain for long-term gain, but Andrea grew increasingly frustrated with the construction process and delays. Michael tried to play mediator, making repeated suggestions.

None appeased Andrea. She would come into the office from court, find furniture rearranged and workers everywhere. They bumped into attorneys, office personnel, and clients. At quitting time, they left everything a mess. Andrea, Michael, and dedicated staff members had to stay late to clean up and locate important files and documents.

With Andrea ready to explode in frustration, Michael took control of the construction project. He declared himself the new construction manager and ordered workers to take his cues. The project would be more organized. Each construction worker would be assigned a specific task, describe how he would complete it, and persuade Michael to sign off. Deadlines were set, and each worker would sign off.

With this new system, the work became more efficient and organized. Construction progressed much faster and smoother. Tasks were completed quicker, with far less clutter and confusion and less disruption of the office staff and attorneys' workflow. Andrea was pleased.

When the buildout was finally completed, Andrea breathed a sigh of relief as the last workman vacated what was now a stunning, state-of-the-art, perfectly functioning law office. One major problem was solved.

Andrea smiled gratefully at Michael, who shrugged, mimicked putting a fork to his mouth, and adopted a hopeful, almost pleading look. Andrea laughed and shook her head, "No."

Everyone celebrated the office's newfound efficiency. Tasks became easier with state-of-the-art electronics and equipment. Every office worker was in synch, but Andrea still felt conflicted.

Pediatric cancer cases became linked to Smith's toy soldiers, and a new batch of defense cases poured in. Michael received multiple cases from Vincent Smith's company, toy soldiers alleged to be a chemical hazard, a choke hazard, or both. Michael expressed concern that someone might turn the litigation into a multi-district class action.

Andrea's intake team received calls about Michigan kids and Vincent Smith's company toy soldiers. She now had ten clients at the claims level. Experts investigated links between toy soldiers, choking incidents, and pediatric cancer. When these cases were filed in court, she and Michael would again be opponents.

Andrea walked into Michael's office one night as both were wrapping up for the day.

"I'm out of here. See you tomorrow."

"Hang on, please. Can we get a bite tonight?"

"I've signed up ten new clients against Smith Toys. Choking and cancer cases—a mixed bag of trouble for your largest client. More are coming in over the next week. We are going to be major adversaries again. Do you think a dinner date is a good idea?" Andrea asked.

"I don't know. Why not? We keep our office life separate and professional. Why can't we have personal lives separate from our professional lives? Look at those talking heads in politics: reds and blues married to each other. They make it work. Why can't we?"

"I don't want to rub it in, but this was your idea, your decision. I wanted to handle cases *together. You* chose this path, remember?"

"The office needed the income. Look at this beautiful place! We couldn't have done it without Smith. Others maintain relationships on opposite sides of the fence, so can we."

"I don't know, Michael. I'm not comfortable with the idea. Not while I represent seriously ill children or the families of deceased children.

What if these families discovered I was seeing the attorney who represents the company responsible for their heartbreak? Not a pretty picture. I can't do it."

She laid a comforting hand on his shoulder and knew he was not happy. However, she would not violate her ethical code. "Give it time. Someday, perhaps."

"I will hold you to that. Someday is better than never. It will be great when it happens."

"I admire your optimism." Andrea backed out and shut his office door. As she reached her car, she saw Michael watching her from his office window. He blew her a kiss and extended his lower lip in an exaggerated pout.

Will it happen, Michael? Can it happen? She hopped in the car and drove away.

CHAPTER SEVENTEEN

Andrea

Spurred by publicity from the insurrection verdict, defective Smith Toy cases flew into Andrea's office. Only one Michigan lawyer now had more cases than Andrea: Bloomfield Hills attorney Zachary Blake, Michigan's self-proclaimed King of Justice.

Andrea admired Blake from afar. He rose to fame on the wheels of a career-making case. He took on the church in a clergy-parishioner sex abuse scandal and uncovered an epic international cover-up. A single trial lawyer brought the Goliath religious institution to its knees with a nine-figure *collectible* verdict, still the highest trial verdict in Michigan history.

Post-verdict, Zack's social justice conquests were legendary. He was the hottest commodity on the Detroit area legal scene. Andrea considered calling him to ask him for advice. Perhaps he'd consider a quasi-partnership, a combined effort, where all cases were filed in generous Wayne County, Smith Toys' headquarters.

On the defense side, Smith Toys and its product liability carrier sent Michael massive amounts of cases in all categories. Smith paid its legal fees promptly, enabling Michael to add staff needed to handle the volume. If business intake continued at this pace, the haunted barn would run out of space.

Andrea was quietly pleased when Vince Smith shocked Michael and retained the Detroit law firm of Taggert, Miles, & Freeman to handle Wayne, Oakland, Macomb, and Genesee County cases. Michael's firm would continue to handle Livingston, Washtenaw, Monroe, and Lenawee County cases.

Michael came into Andrea's office to whine about Smith's back-stabbing decision.

"I've worked my ass off for that guy and his company. How can he do this to me?"

"Is he still sending you a huge volume of cases?"

"Yes."

"Is he paying you?"

"Yes."

"On time?"

"Like clockwork," Michael calmed.

"So, what are you complaining about? There are thousands of cases across the country. One firm can't handle all."

"I get that, but Taggert? Smith must know I hate Taggert."

"What does she care? This is the big leagues. Smith is concerned only with his company and investors. He has no desire to referee a petty squabble between two lawyers.

"Taggert is the largest defense firm in Michigan and one of the top ten in the country. Yet, Smith came to our little barn and retained *you* first. I'd call that a win."

"Taggert's in Wayne County. The bulk of the cases were filed there. All cases will be consolidated in Wayne if class-action status is granted. Taggert will be lead counsel. It sucks to be me."

"Keep your head down and handle the southwestern clients to the best of your ability." She saw he was furious, but the client is the boss in the attorney-client relationship. The *client* dictates terms.

"There are only two things you can do."

"What are those?"

"Grin and bear it or terminate the relationship and renounce all that blood money."

"Funny, Kramer. I expected a bit more support from you."

"I'm sorry you feel that way. I've given you solid, practical advice. We're on opposite sides, remember. What did you expect?"

"I'm not sure. More."

"Sorry. Good advice is all I have."

Michael

Michael was angry at Andrea. When he sought her opinion and advice, he expected unconditional support. Instead, he got the unbridled truth. Over time, he came to understand her wisdom and Smith's reasoning. A joint defense of claims *was* the most expeditious way of handling the litigation. As Michael expected, however, the decision not only put the two lawyers on a collision course, but Taggert landed the plum Metropolitan Detroit assignment.

Metro Detroit's tri-county (Wayne, Oakland, and Macomb) area was enormous compared to the rest of Michigan. Most of the state's population lived in those three counties. Taggert would be billing far more hours for Smith than Michael.

That was life in the big city. Smith Toys was headquartered in Detroit, and Michael was confident that lawyers who got their hands on Smith Toy cases would file their lawsuits in Wayne County. Andrea's sound advice helped Michael realize he had no choice but to hold his nose and work with Taggert for the client's benefit. He was raking in the dough, busy with the southwestern counties. Hourly billing for Smith Toys exceeded mid-six figures and would skyrocket once cases were filed in court.

Andrea

Andrea's and Zachary Blake's firm were taking in Smith Toy cases in numbers that dwarfed every other Michigan law firm. For expediency, practicality, and easy money, lawyers referred cases to the two law firms, according to client location. Blake's firm handled the northeast, while Andrea's captured the southwest.

On a bright, sunny day in Saline, Andrea sat at her desk, preparing her template for another client's lawsuit against Smith Toys. Her desk phone rang. She pressed a button on the intercom.

"Zachary Blake is on the line," her receptionist announced. Andrea shivered. She planned to contact Blake but had no idea she was even on *his* radar screen. She picked up the receiver.

"Andrea Kramer."

"Andrea! Nice to meet you on the phone! Have we met?"

"We met once, a few years ago, at a seminar."

"Oh? Which one?" Zack asked.

"Auto-neg and no-fault, I believe, long before the priest case. Things have changed since then—for both of us."

"They certainly have. Nice verdict for Longbow. Those sons-of-bitches deserved the ass-kicking you laid on them. I've got some insurrection cases, but nothing like Longbow. Your verdict sure greased the skids. Congratulations, *Mazel Tov*, as we say in Yiddish!" Zack exclaimed.

"Thank you. Same to you for your amazing run of success. How may I help you today?" Andrea got down to business.

"We seem to be *the* two Michigan lawyers tapped to handle Smith Toy cases. Let's turn the matter into a multi-district case and share lead attorney status. What do you say? We can discuss fee splits and client control later. What do you think?"

"Work with Zachary Blake on the biggest cases in my practice? I'm honored!" Andrea gasped. She had to be honest. "I'm strapped for cash, though. I still haven't collected fees on Longbow. Will that be a problem?"

"No. Consolidating these cases will save us both a ton of money. How about this? I'll advance costs. You pay your fair share if you get the Longbow money before the toy cases are resolved. If you don't, my firm gets a slightly larger percentage at the end of the case. We'll call it interest on advanced file costs. If, for some reason, the cases fail, we split the costs after your Longbow fees come in. Sound fair?"

"More than fair. This solves a lot of problems for me," Andrea replied.

"Do you work with an investigative firm?"

"No. I had a small country practice before Longbow. I haven't yet cultivated those types of resources. Do you have someone?"

"Micah Love, Love Investigations. Micah helped me crack all those famous cases. You will *love* Micah. He can be a bit crass, but he keeps things loose and is the best PI in the state.

"He and the clients deserve all the praise. I'm only their conduit in the courtroom."

"Be you ever so humble. Give me a break. Take credit where credit is due. You have done historic work. You make me proud to be a trial lawyer, and I'm honored you thought of me. If Micah is who you say he is, he will crack this case," Andrea consented.

"Smith Toys will do everything possible to prevent the truth from seeing the light of day. I wouldn't be surprised if Vince Smith himself bought a giant document shredder for the occasion," Andrea advised.

"You know the man?" Zack sounded surprised.

"Met him once. He came into the office seeking representation. As you can imagine, defending a corporate wrongdoer is not my thing. However, I share space with Michael O'Hara. I'm sure you know him. He agreed to represent Smith. He's handling a ton of Smith defense cases, especially on my side of the state. You've probably seen his name on some of your pleadings," Andrea advised.

"I know Michael well. We've been on opposite sides before. Talented guy. It was his ass you kicked in the Longbow litigation, right?"

"Correct."

"He's not easy to beat. We'll have to rehash that war story one of these days. Will the fact that you two share an office be a problem?"

"No. We've worked out the logistics, and he's honorable."

"Very well, then. I'll have my people draft an agreement, and we'll set up a meeting to sign everything. Good?"

"More than good. You've taken a huge load off my plate."

"Glad I could help. Besides, I need another steady hand on this litigation. I followed the Longbow trial—and snuck into the courtroom a few times. You are a terrific litigator. I'm proud to team up with someone of your caliber. Taggert and O'Hara will have their hands full. Talk soon?"

"You bet. Thanks for calling and for the generous proposal. I look forward to working with you and your team."

"Likewise, bye."

"Goodbye."

He watched me in court! Andrea was pumped. A litigation partnership with Zachary Blake—*watch out, O'Hara! Here we come!*

CHAPTER EIGHTEEN

Andrea

Andrea and her administrative staff met in the conference room to review protocol for the multi-district litigation and coordinate workflow with Zachary Blake and other outside counsel.

Michael walked into the office. A meeting was in progress, with coffee, orange juice, bagels, and donuts. He pranced into the conference room with a smile on his face.

"Did I miss a memo about an office meeting?" He chirped.

"No, you didn't," Andrea replied. "This is about the multidistrict plaintiff litigation against your client, Smith Toys. You weren't invited—I'm sure you understand."

"Completely," Michael acknowledged. "May I grab an orange juice and a bagel?"

"Help yourself. When this meeting is over, I need to talk to you. Will you be around this morning?"

"Yes, I'm around all day. Come in when you're ready," Michael replied. He grabbed his food and walked out the door.

"You haven't told him about the multi-district litigation agreement with Blake?" Andrea's chief paralegal inquired.

"No. I wanted to brief all of you on future protocol. We will assign two teams, one for the defense and the other for the plaintiff. We will have strict no-contact and no-sharing rules and maintain discretion and client confidence. Michael's new hires, in addition to Sabrina, Adrienne, and Jennifer, will work the defense side of things. The rest of you are with me. Any questions?"

"What if we don't want to work the defense side?" Adrienne wondered. "I don't see myself helping a toy company poison or choke children to death."

"Same here," Sabrina spouted. "How about you, Jennifer?"

"I'm Switzerland. This is a job. I don't get to choose sides. I'm comfortable on either side of the litigation. This is a *law office*, not a crusade," Jennifer advised.

Andrea cringed at her response. Jennifer was correct in her analysis, but her cold, almost robotic response did not sit well. *How can anyone be so dispassionate? Does this woman have any feelings at all?*

"When this meeting is over, I will be talking to Michael. We'll discuss future staffing and client privilege issues. Michael might want to go outside the firm for staffing," Andrea suggested. "Let's wait and see."

Andrea sat in Michael O'Hara's office an hour later, dropping the Zachary Blake collaboration bombshell. The cases would be consolidated into a multi-district class action filed in Wayne County. Andrea would handle the southwestern clients. Zack would take the tri-county area. Select Michigan Association for Justice attorneys would receive referrals in counties north of Lansing. Out-of-state cases would be coordinated by the Blake law office and handed off to American Association for Justice members with multidistrict case experience. Michael expressed displeasure with the news.

"That means all Michigan cases will be pursued in Wayne County. Why would Smith need me if he has a firm like Taggert to handle the whole class? This really sucks."

"I'm sorry, but I had to do what is best for the class of *plaintiffs* in this case. A collaboration with Zachary Blake is in the best interests of the class," Andrea concluded.

"I get that, but it still sucks to be me."

"Don't sell yourself short. Vincent Smith likes you. You're more talented than anyone at the Taggert firm. You'll have a place at the table when all is said and done."

"Taking orders from Stu Taggert again, the prick who fired me. Sounds fun, like I said, it sucks to be me."

"Who's to say you will be taking orders? Perhaps you'll be *giving* them. Ever think of that?" Andrea suggested.

"I love how you try to make sweet lemonade from sour lemons," Michael chuckled.

"That's a nice thing to say. Thank you."

"I have no choice but to put my head down, plow into the work, and let the chips fall where they may. May the best man win," Michael declared.

"That's the spirit," Andrea cheered.

"What about a lunch or dinner date? How do you and I handle these new developments?" Michael asked.

"Nothing changes. We maintain separate divisions and assignments. Client confidentiality remains strictly enforced. We're both professionals," she insisted. "I'm still considering lunch or dinner."

At that moment, a loud clap of thunder shook the office.

"Whoa!" Michael looked around. "Storm coming."

"Weather forecasters predicted a storm, but this is earlier than expected. I sent the staff home early to stack up on food and supplies. They predict lots of rain, wind overnight, and a possible tornado. I'm concerned."

By five in the evening, Saline looked like a ghost town. Almost every downtown business had shuttered. Residents hunkered down in their homes, waiting for the storm to hit.

Andrea sat alone in her office after five, working at her desk. She chatted on the phone and pecked away at a keyboard.

She sensed someone watching, looked up, and caught Michael staring through his office window. She stopped and stared back.

Michael embraced the moment and waved to her with a smile. She smiled, waved back, and returned to her computer screen. Light music played over the intercom.

The sky grew dark. Five-thirty in the afternoon looked eerily like eight in the evening. A warning tone came over the intercom, replacing the music. An electronic voice announced a severe thunderstorm warning. Suddenly, the office power went out.

An eerie silence enveloped the office. Birds went silent. The leaves stopped fluttering. Outside, two kids ignored the warning, playing in a nearby park, laughing and chasing each other, oblivious to the danger. Michael left the building and ran across the street to the park. Andrea watched him approach the two boys and send them on their way.

What a sweet and brave thing to do!

Michael returned to the office and locked the front door. He glanced at Andrea's closed-door office as he returned to his. Andrea rose and walked over.

"The power's out—nothing we can do. We should get out of here before the storm hits. That was a nice thing you did for those kids."

"Crazy kids! Do they have a death wish? They might get hit by lightning! Where are their parents?"

"Indeed. But 'Uncle Michael' took care of the situation and set them straight," she laughed.

A massive clap of thunder interrupted their light banter, and a lightning bolt lit up the dark sky.

"Shit!" Andrea jumped at nature's sudden fury. The wind picked up—once still trees swayed. A few drops fell from the sky, which darkened even more. A ferocious storm suddenly lashed the small downtown business district.

Wind velocity increased, and debris blew everywhere, slamming into buildings and cracking a few windows. Trees bowed dangerously in the stiff wind. The streetlights were out since the power was out, making the storm appear even more ominous. Michael turned to Andrea.

"This storm is some serious shit," he muttered. "I better make sure the building is secure."

"I agree, but how are you going to do that?"

"I'll be right back." He left her alone in the office. Andrea heard the front door open and shut. She walked to the window and observed Michael outside, fighting the pouring rain and strong winds. He checked the siding, moved to the outside windows and doors, and ensured the outdoor storage unit was clamped down and locked. When he finished, he returned to the office, soaking wet.

Andrea looked up at him, her eyes shining with admiration. It was a small act that demonstrated a level of care and concern that she did not believe she deserved. The gesture meant a lot to her.

"Oh my God, Michael! What a sweet thing to do! Dangerous, dumb, but very sweet. Thank you. Look at you! You're soaking wet! The last time I saw you like this, you had ginger ale all over your face."

"Funny, Kramer," He smiled and looked down at his soaked clothing. "Just trying to help," he crooned. "Isn't that what partners do?"

"No! Well . . . maybe the nutty ones," she laughed.

The storm continued to rage outside. The rain came down in sheets. The building shook from the strength of the wind. Debris flew into the air and pounded the siding. Michael and Andrea stood, side by side, five feet from the window, looking out in fear as the storm intensified. Andrea turned to Michael.

"I'm not sure it's safe here. This is an old building. Do you think we should get out of here?" Andrea suggested.

"Good thought, I guess. But where would we go?"

"My place is just up the street."

"How far?"

"A block and a half."

Michael shrugged and nodded. "Let's go."

They walked out onto the porch. Andrea turned to lock the door. The wind was so strong it was difficult to stand. Michael grabbed her hand and pulled her close as they ventured into the teeth of the storm. They struggled down the street, dodging dangerous flying debris, wind, and rain beating against them.

Andrea questioned their decision to leave the office. Michael held her close. She felt the warmth of his body, wrapping her up with one side of his open coat. They reached Andrea's apartment and collapsed on the floor, drenched and exhausted. Michael turned to Andrea and laughed, his teeth glimmering, his blue eyes crinkling at the corners.

"Well, that's a story we can tell our grandchildren. You are one brave lady. A screw loose maybe, but very brave."

Andrea circled a finger around her ear and temple to signify her loose screw. The two of them laughed out loud at the gesture.

Andrea sat upright and wiped the rain from her face, relieved to be safe. She turned to Michael and wiped his face with her opposite, dryer hand. Their eyes met. She nodded, silently acknowledging her gratitude for his safe harbor in the storm.

They continued to sit on the apartment floor, heads down, clothes rumpled and wet, wondering what to do next.

"Andrea? Can we talk about the Smith situation? I want us to be good together," Michael pleaded.

"I understand completely, Michael. Do you want to talk this out *here*, on the floor, dripping wet?" She wondered.

"Yes, Andrea, I do. I care about you . . . and your feelings. But this client—"

"Is perfect," she finished his sentence. "It's what you do, I get it. Smith sure seems like the golden goose. But he pits us against each other. Surely you see that."

"Nothing we can't handle. We've done it before and managed to develop a relationship," he argued.

"Relationship? We fought like cats and dogs. I won, you lost. You lost your job, went into a tailspin, and landed here. As I recall, you *stalked* me, Michael."

"Legally, my conduct did not rise to the level of stalking."

"What would you call it?"

"I'm not sure I want to continue this conversation," he retreated.

"Why not? It's a conversation we need to have. Will our relationship be landlord-tenant, suitemates, partners, or something more? Smith doesn't exactly get us off to a great start."

"You're willing to explore 'something more?'" He hand-signed quotation marks.

"I didn't say that. I said we weren't off to a good start," she grumbled. *I shouldn't have offered him an olive branch or rented him the office space.*

"We're adults. We can manage two things at the same time. I need to know that you will be okay with the Smith litigation. I'll move out if that's what you want," Michael offered.

"Is that what *you* want?"

"No! Andrea—" He turned to her, lifted her chin, and looked into her eyes. She tried to divert hers. "Look at me, please?" He pleaded. She raised her eyes to meet his.

"I want more," he confessed.

"More?"

"More." He leaned forward. Their lips met in a short, soft kiss. Andrea turned away.

"Michael? Do you think—" He again leaned forward and kissed her again. This time, she did not turn away. *How do I feel? Should I stop this here and now?*

A warm vibration reached her inner core—she wanted him. She wanted him to hold her and to feel his skin against hers.

She hesitated again. "The office, Michael." He kissed her. "The Smith cases." He tickled her neck with his tongue. "We're opponents again."

Michael pressed his lips into hers, reached behind her back, unhooked her bra, and brushed his lips gently across her breasts. She shivered. He returned to her face, holding her cheeks in his hands.

"Are you cold? You're shivering."

"Two reasons," she smiled. "Hold me." She removed his shirt. His chest heaved. His skin was hot.

"Better?" he asked.

"Much."

"It's probably warmer under the covers," he suggested.

"Why, Mr. O'Hara. I do think you're trying to seduce me," she giggled.

"Whatever gave you that idea?" He stood. The tension in the air crackled as Andrea reached up and unbuckled his pants. As they fell to the floor, he stepped out of them. Her fingertips danced along the waistband of his underwear, causing the intended reaction. He reached down and gently pulled her up along his body, igniting sparks in every nerve ending.

He unhooked her skirt, and it fluttered to the floor before he gently lifted her into his arms and silently carried her into the bedroom. Soft music played in the room. Michael gently laid her on the bed and joined her on the other side. Snuggled under the warm covers, Andrea pressed her body into his, feeling the warmth of his skin against hers.

His hands gently caressed her face and began to move down to her neck, tracing small circles and sending shivers down her spine. Andrea wrapped her arms around him, clinging onto him tightly as if to never let go.

Andrea's body wanted him, but her mind still resisted. She couldn't chase the case or her clients from her mind. Michael pulled away.

"What's wrong?" he asked.

"Should we be here, like this, at this moment? There is so much at stake for both of us."

"Should we deny our feelings?" He asked, holding her close and kissing her forehead. "We're professionals. We can separate our personal and professional lives."

"Maybe you can. I'm not sure about me."

"Won't you even try? I've waited, no, *longed* for this moment, probably from the time we first met on Longbow."

"I felt it too, Michael."

"We've established office protocol and created appropriate separation. We can do that in our personal lives. I have *feelings* for you, Andrea."

"Michael . . ." she whispered his name. He kissed her again. She felt herself melt . . . give in to the passion of the moment. *It's been a long time since I felt like this.*

Michael held her close. "I want you, Andrea. Let this go," he pleaded.

It felt right to lay with him, hold him in her arms, make love to him. She gave more of herself to him and tossed apprehension aside. Their mouths separated, and they gazed at each other. Michael kissed her cheek, moved down to her shoulders, and continued downward. Andrea relaxed, slowly succumbing to passion.

"You're okay with us being together for moments at a time but not during discovery and trial?" Her voice cracked. She felt her body burn with desire as Michael's lips probed her body.

He lifted his head from under the covers to face her. "Okay? No. Willing to try? Yes. Do you want me to stop?"

Andrea paused. "No," she responded. "Continue, please," she chirped. She wanted to be with him. She'd think about the case, the clients, and the office after the storm. He pulled her closer. *Michael* . . . was all that mattered at that moment in time.

Later, they lay next to each other. Andrea rested her head on Michael's chest and twirled his chest hairs in her fingers.

"All I wanted was a damn *drink*," he laughed, kissing her head.

"Are you complaining? We can go back to being *that* couple if you want," she teased.

"No way," he gasped. "This was way better than a drink."

"I'd forgotten it could be like this," she murmured. "This was wonderful, Michael. *You* were wonderful."

"I haven't felt this way with anyone for a long time," he confessed.

Everything disappeared in these tender moments: the office, the contentious litigation, and the possible conflict of interest. Andrea looked up at him.

"Thank you for protecting me from the storm. I've enjoyed every moment with you."

"Want more protection?" Michael gave her the Groucho eye waggle. Andrea felt safe and secure. Much later, they fell asleep in each other's arms as the storm raged outside Andrea's apartment.

CHAPTER NINETEEN

Andrea stirred, forced one eye open, and looked around her bedroom. Michael was gone. *What time is it?*

She rose from the bed and went to the window. Sunlight poured in when Andrea cracked open the shutters. The sun shone in a cloudless sky. Puddles of water dotted a wet main street, with debris scattered everywhere. Cleanup from the storm would be difficult and expensive. She wondered if there might have been a tornado.

Suddenly self-conscious of her body, she strutted to the bathroom and grabbed her robe from the hook on the back of the door. The mirror was steamy. Michael must have showered moments ago. *Where is he?*

She smelled coffee and heard sounds coming from the kitchen. Venturing toward it, she smelled bacon and heard sizzling on the hot stove. She walked into the kitchen to find Michael, fully clothed for work, stirring eggs in a small bowl. The blissfully domestic scene delighted her. She stood and watched until he sensed her presence and looked up.

"Well, well. Good morning, sunshine! How did you sleep?" He asked.

"Good morning to you. Like a baby. I was . . . exhausted . . . from all . . . the activity. What's this?"

"Breakfast. Want some coffee?"

"I would *love* some coffee. What time is it?"

"Seven-thirty. The power is still out at the office. They're working to restore the downtown business district as we speak."

"But it's only a couple blocks away."

"Different grid, I suppose. How do you like your eggs?"

"I'll have them the same way you have them. What are you, a short-order cook?"

"It's my pleasure to spoil my favorite girl," he smiled.

Andrea cringed. *His favorite girl? We are on opposite sides of a huge case. I can't be his favorite girl. I've got to nip this in the bud.*

"Cut the crap, O'Hara. Breakfast is great. Last night was wonderful. But we are on opposite sides of a big case. Let's keep things casual. I can't be your favorite girl," she muttered.

"Simmer down. I read you loud and clear last night. Total separation between personal life and business life. Total separation at the office between the defense and the plaintiff. I get it. Not to worry—the office is closed. We lost power, remember? We are still on personal time. How do you like your eggs?"

Andrea retreated. "Scrambled is fine." For the rest of the morning, the atmosphere was tentative.

"I kinda-sorta lied about sleeping like a baby," she confessed with a whisper. "I kept waking, wondering—did we make a mistake?"

His eyes darkened. His face contorted, almost to a scowl. "I don't think so. Did we?"

She was silent for a moment, trying to gauge where they were and what their next steps might be. She had succumbed to passion and crossed a line. They were co-workers, equal in every way but one. *It's my name on the door.*

Andrea felt an inherent responsibility as the firm owner. Michael was building his practice side-by-side with hers. At some point, might they be *competing* for cases?

"We need to talk about last night and the future."

"I thought actions spoke louder than words," he snickered.

Andrea blushed. "Can you get your mind out of bed and consider business for a moment?"

"Sorry, sure."

"I have certain aspirations. I'm trying to grow a plaintiff's practice. I want the office and both of us to be successful. I don't want to hinder your practice, but I am having difficulty figuring out how opposite practices co-exist in the same space. It strikes me as an uneasy balance."

"I'm not sure what you're getting at," Michael winced.

"You're a good businessman. I prefer the attorney side of things. I'd love to have you manage the business side and give you autonomy to do so. But my brand and pedigree are sacrosanct. The Kramer firm is a *plaintiff* firm. I must consider my reputation."

"Understood."

"I'm not sure you do."

"I took Vince Smith on as a client, the opposite of what you would have done. We will be on opposing sides. You want to be a team. How can we be a team if we're always opponents? Does that size up how you're feeling?"

"Yes. I want us to be a *team*, personally and professionally. Perhaps that's a selfish ambition. I have no right to demand you switch sides. Yet, somehow, I feel we are destined to work together. How do we continue our collaboration and ensure that your success is not hindered by mine?"

"Are you asking a hypothetical, or do you want my opinion?" Michael asked.

"I'm not sure, both?"

"We have feelings for each other. At least, I have feelings for you. May I presume they are mutual?"

"Yes."

"Good, glad we cleared that up," he laughed nervously. "We've crossed a particular line in our relationship. There is no going back, right? We enjoy each other's company—why can't we create a business relationship or partnership in an environment of mutual respect, collaboration, and understanding? I think we can do it. I can manage the business and handle Smith. You concentrate on your plaintiffs' practice."

"I'm willing to do whatever it takes to make that happen, so long as I don't have to compromise my principles," she warned.

"You are a trial lawyer, a plaintiffs' trial lawyer. I understand and respect your wishes in that regard. A part of me longs to be where you are, but I haven't notched an eight-figure verdict. The Smith representation is too important to my bottom line. When it's over, we can reassess. Sound good?"

"The building lease and office administration will be one entity you manage and maintain. Our two offices will be maintained separately as entities two and three. You manage yours. I'll manage mine. We'll share staff," Andrea concluded.

"Exactly," Michael agreed. "So long as we don't return to where we were before. I like where we're at now," he grinned.

"Me too."

"The personal relationship doesn't have to affect the business, our practices, the building, or staff management," he confirmed.

"The future seems bright," she agreed. "I don't want to create any barriers to success for either of us. I'll stick to the practice and stay out of the business end of things, giving you room to lead. By sharing staff and keeping everyone in the loop, we should be able to make this work. Combining our strengths can make us a powerful joint force."

"Exactly. Let's give having it all a try."

"Amen to that."

Andrea had always been a team player. Working with her friends was her favorite activity, even as a child. It was time to apply that same mentality to Michael and the business. She had faith that the two of them could create something unique. It was time for Andrea and Michael to redefine their partnership and advance the law practice.

She flashed to their intimate, beautiful moments the day before. *I don't want to stop feeling this way.* She hoped things would work out if they continued talking and sharing ideas. It was time for them to move forward together and ensure the mutual success of their business venture.

She strolled to the coffee maker and refilled their cups. She brought Michael his coffee, sat across from him, and smiled.

"To the future," she declared.

"Here, here," he chirped. "To the future."

The coffee steamed between them as they talked, each catching up on the other's thoughts and ideas. Michael quickly morphed into business mode, the man he'd been before they'd made love. After some time, Andrea felt a renewed sense of faith in their partnership. Michael seemed as passionate and ambitious as before, willing to work with her to ensure the business thrived. She sensed that both were ready to move forward together. *We'll create something amazing.* She felt they would bridge whatever gap stood between them, a refreshing feeling that gave her hope for an exciting journey together.

Andrea harbored one fear, though. *What if Michael grows bored with the novelty of small-town life and wants to move back to Detroit?* What would she do then? She kept that question to herself and buried it deep in her heart. Where was her insecurity coming from?

She wanted to trust and believe in Michael, but something held her back. She could not control what others decided to do, only *her* behavior. No matter what happened, she knew she would be there for him, come what may.

CHAPTER TWENTY

Michael

The power was fully restored that afternoon, and Saline returned to normal. A few weeks went by, and the town recovered its peaceful bliss. This weekend morning, the air was crisp, with a slight bite from the chill of the previous evening. Birds chirped and fluttered around, searching for food, while children ran up and down the street playing tag. Onlookers enjoyed coffee on porches and watched life pass by. Cars drove slowly, in no hurry to get anywhere, as the sun shone bright and warm. It was a morning like any other—peaceful, tranquil, and without incident—until things suddenly changed.

First, Michael heard screeching tires. He looked out his window and witnessed a semi-truck broadside a small, older model sedan. The crash shattered the quiet of the morning and replaced it with panic, fear, and dread.

Michael jumped into the fray, pulling Andrea along. He pulled out his cell phone and called 9-1-1.

"Good morning, 9-1-1. May I help you?"

"There's been a terrible auto and semi-truck crash," Michael shouted into the receiver. He gave the operator the cross streets, his name, and office address. He and Andrea ran toward the crushed blue sedan. He called over a couple of onlookers.

"Are you okay, ma'am?" he asked the elderly driver.

"I-I I think so," she slurred her words, semi-conscious. Blood trickled down both cheeks from deep lacerations. "I'm stuck. Please, get me out of here!"

"What's your name?" Michael wanted to keep her talking.

"Emma Simpson."

"How old are you?" Michael asked.

"Never ask a woman her age," Emma smiled weakly.

Michael chuckled. "Sorry." He covered his mouth with his hand and winked at Emma.

"We're going to get you out. Stay with me, please." He turned to Andrea, standing behind him, and motioned her over. He hovered over Emma.

"Emma, this is my friend Andrea. Maybe she'll tell you how old she is." Andrea looked confused.

"I'm eighty," Emma admitted.

Two onlookers stood by, ready to contribute. Michael turned to them.

"Can you give me a hand?" he asked. "We need to free her, somehow, and pull her out of this seat. It's dangerous."

"I'll try to pry open the door," one man offered. "We may need some tools."

"We may have to wait for EMS," the other suggested.

"Let's give it a try," Michael decided.

Andrea awkwardly re-directed traffic as Michael and the others tried to pry open the driver's side door. More helpers joined the effort. Gasoline odor permeated the air. The old car moaned and creaked while dark liquid trickled from every orifice. Every volunteer raced against time to free the woman from a vehicle they believed might explode at any moment. Michael and the other volunteers did everything they could to save the woman's life. From time to time, Michael returned to Emma's side and smiled.

"Piece of cake, Emma. We'll have you out of here with a couple of yanks and tugs. How do you feel?"

"Not so hot. I'm getting woozy."

"Stay with me, dear. EMS is on its way."

After what seemed like an eternity, sirens were heard in the background. Emergency vehicles arrived at the scene.

"What's the situation?" The team leader demanded.

"We lifted the steering wheel and moved the seat back. The steering wheel compressed her chest. She lost consciousness a few times. She's breathing better now," Michael advised.

"Thanks for your assistance. You guys move aside now. Let's get her out of the car, check her condition, and transfer her into the ambulance."

Michael turned to Emma. "EMS is here. The pros are going to take over, okay?"

"Will you stay with me?" Emma pleaded.

"Of course, if that's what you want." Michael and the volunteers stepped aside, pleased to be relieved by the professionals. Emergency personnel and paramedics took over, placing a cervical collar around Mrs. Simpson's neck, carefully moving her sideways, extricating her, and lifting her out of her vehicle.

Moments after paramedics loaded Emma Simpson into the transport vehicle, Michael smelled an even more pungent odor of gasoline. A loud bang sounded. Michael felt intense heat behind him. He turned to see Emma's car erupt in flames.

Molten debris shot into the air and landed on the pavement. Michael, Andrea, and other volunteers dodged falling debris. Miraculously, no one was hit. The old car continued to sizzle.

"Get these people out of here," a policeman ordered.

"Move it, people," another directed.

"This way!" Michael directed pedestrians away, like a traffic cop. He pointed to the sidewalk about twenty-five yards from the burning car. The scene was chaotic and surreal. Pieces of metal and glass were strewn around Mrs. Simpson's car. Fire danced around the front hood. A fire truck arrived, and firefighters jumped from the vehicle. They sprayed flame retardant foam at the burning vehicle. Paramedics rushed Emma to a nearby hospital.

A police captain walked over to the lightly damaged semi-truck resting on the opposite side of the street. The driver sat motionless inside the vehicle. Michael ventured over to listen and observe.

"Are you okay, sir?" the captain inquired.

"I'm okay. I'm just shaken up. I-I never saw her. Where 'n hell she come from?" The man slurred his speech.

"Did you see the stop sign, sir?"

"Stop sign?"

"Have you been drinking, sir?" The cop demanded.

"It's morning."

"That wasn't my question, sir. Have you been drinking?"

"I may have had a beer or two."

"Step out of the vehicle," the cop ordered.

"My back hurts," the man grimaced, suddenly in severe pain.

"Can you move?"

"I'm not sure," he faltered.

"Let's try." The cop helped him out of the vehicle.

"Follow my finger, please?" He moved his index finger back and forth in the man's face.

"Extend your arms and slowly bring them forward to touch your nose. One arm at a time, please?" The man struggled to comply.

"I'm having difficulty holding my arms up," he slurred.

"Take nine steps, please, heel-to-toe. Walk a straight line." The man stumbled trying to comply. "Now, come on back the same way." The man almost tripped over his own feet.

Michael watched in silence. He knew this routine all too well. *This guy should have a lawyer.* He hesitated to intervene. *The bastard deserves what he gets.*

"One more test. Stand on one leg," the cop directed.

"I'm tired. I think I have internal injuries. I need to get to a hospital," the man whined.

"Let's get you to a hospital," the cop concurred. He removed a pair of handcuffs from his belt.

"What are those for?" the man demanded, wide-eyed.

"I'm placing you under arrest, sir. You have the right to remain silent—"

Police officers questioned bystanders, including Michael and Andrea.

Michael ran his hands through his hair in disbelief as he and Andrea stood inside, watching the aftermath of the accident outside. Saline Fire and Rescue personnel were in the final stages of putting out the fire. Michael turned to Andrea, a worried expression on his face.

"Holy shit! That's what happens when you mix driving with alcohol."

Andrea shook her head. "Horrible! I hope Emma is okay."

"The paramedic said she has an excellent chance," Michael replied.

"Thanks to you and your co-heroes," Andrea praised.

"Do you know her?"

"We're acquainted. She lives around the corner on the next block," she pointed. "She was probably on her way home."

"Did you see the crash? I can't believe—" Michael's thoughts turned to how life can change in an instant. He scanned the crowd around the site, observed individuals, and gauged conscious and subconscious responses to the accident.

"According to witnesses, the semi-truck driver blew the stop sign going at least fifteen miles per hour over the speed limit," Andrea advised.

Emergency vehicles left the scene. A tow truck driver and his assistant handled the charred remains of Emma Simpson's car. A second, police-owned tow truck team dealt with the semi. Gawkers cried and consoled each other. Shock and sadness hung in the air.

Michael felt suddenly overcome with guilt and sorrow. *This might have been me!* Andrea observed his demeanor, put her arm on his shoulder, and gently herded him toward the office.

"Let's go back to work," she suggested.

They returned to the haunted barn, memories of the accident acting as fresh salt on a lingering wound. Michael tried to focus on work. His thoughts kept returning to the alcohol-impaired driver and how a typical day suddenly became tragic. He settled into his desk chair, stared at a blank computer screen, and silently vowed to work the program and live every day as if it might be his last day on earth. He didn't know it yet, but another storm was brewing, this one in his mind, ready to alter his psyche again.

Andrea

"Does anyone know how Mrs. Simpson is doing?" Andrea inquired the following morning.

"She's still in the hospital. I called this morning. I'm not family. They won't provide details, but she's alive. The news says she's in serious condition," the office manager advised.

"What about the truck driver?" a paralegal wondered.

"Minor cuts and bruises, symptoms equivalent to post-traumatic stress. He's been arrested and booked on suspicion of DUI," the office manager replied.

"I've got post-traumatic stress from hearing that horrible collision and seeing poor Emma trapped in that car," moaned another clerical worker.

"Do you know Mrs. Simpson?" Andrea asked.

"Yes. Why? Is there a case?"

"That's not why I asked. I wondered if anyone had notified her family. Does she have children or grandchildren in the area?"

"Yes. I can get ahold of her daughter. I'll mention the office. Maybe we can pick up a case."

Andrea flushed. "Again, that's not why I asked."

Michael intervened. "But go ahead and ask. Emma could not do better than Andrea. We all know that."

Andrea knew that in moments of chaos, good citizens must strive to remain kind and care for each other, no matter what. Quick action by Michael and others in assisting Mrs. Simpson saved her life.

***

Three weeks after her horrific accident, Emma Simpson retained Andrea to sue the Remington Truck Company, the owner of the truck that caused her accident. Ms. Simpson spent a week and a half in the hospital, suffering from a crushed sternum, numerous broken bones, a collapsed lung, and facial lacerations. Remington employed the negligent driver and was a deep-pocket defendant with a sizeable insurance policy. It was one more huge case for the Kramer Law Office.

Judge Daniel Kolber drew all Smith Toy cases in litigation. Andrea and Zack Blake celebrated the draw. Michael and Taggert greeted the judicial assignment with far less enthusiasm. Both teams considered the experienced judge to be to the left of center. He placed the cases on the so-called 'rocket docket' and expected the parties to agree on trial dates. Andrea believed the cases were headed for class action certification.

Andrea continued to see Michael after office hours and in romantic interludes during lunch hours.

"Where are the lovebirds?" a clerical worker asked one day.

"Where do you think? It's lunchtime. You know where they go and what they do for lunch," a paralegal snickered.

Andrea knew the staff talked behind their backs. At first, she was embarrassed. She discussed it with Michael.

"Are we setting a bad example?"

"Why? We're consenting adults. We don't fool around at the office. We're respectful of others. I love being with you. I especially enjoy *making* love to you."

"I feel the same."

"What *should* people who have feelings for each other be doing?"

"You're suggesting that they're going to talk anyway, so why not give them something to talk about?"

"Exactly."

Andrea looked into Michael's eyes. He took her breath away. Her heart thumped in her chest. She believed they were stronger together and able to rise to *any* challenge.

During their moments of intimacy, Andrea delighted in her closeness with Michael. Years of placing her education and career ahead of her desires caused her to question her self-worth. Michael brought her comfort and pleasure and made her feel desired again.

His warmth filled her with deep contentment, an emotion she clung to and refused to let go. She felt the heartbeat of long-sought passion she never knew existed. The feeling was like no other: euphoria mixed with awe.

"Do you ever wonder?" she once asked Michael.

"Wonder what?"

"How you ever lived without me? I wonder that of you. My life was exciting, a new practice and sudden success, but an emotional void existed. You filled it. I can no longer imagine life without you."

"Ditto."

"Ditto? Who are you? Patrick Swayze?" She puffed out her lower lip and pouted.

"I feel the same way, Andrea. I can no longer imagine life without you."

"That's better."

"Thank you."

"You're welcome."

"I trust you, Andrea," he whispered. His words were nothing, yet *everything*.

Slowly, her fears of intimacy with Michael evaporated. She realized her best moments involved him, thoughts of him, feelings for him, and his presence in her life. *I might be in love.*

Would there be more? Neither of them could imagine what lay ahead.

CHAPTER TWENTY-ONE

Andrea

The Smith Toys litigation reached a fever pitch. These days, Andrea had little time for anything but what she referred to as "the case."

Emma Simpson's case and others were progressing, with associate attorneys and paralegals taking the lead. Like Andrea, these young associates and paralegals were learning the meaning of trial by fire not too long ago.

Andrea continued to blossom, now under the watchful eye of Zachary Blake. She also reaped the benefits of Micah Love's stellar investigative work. Micah identified and developed several company whistleblowers. These parents of small children were providing damning testimony that Vincent Smith was not only aware his toys caused illness and choked young children; he actively covered up these defects.

Former Smith employees and previous litigants testified that records of prior cases, settlements, and trials were hidden or destroyed. Smith covered up previous settlements with non-disclosure agreements and court-ordered seals. Nuisance value settlements or losses were the only cases that populated any court records available to the public. Damning safety engineer reports disappeared, replaced by sanitized versions, the best expert opinions money could buy.

But none of Smith's deceptions prevented Micah Love from uncovering the truth. Plaintiff-by-plaintiff, witness-by-witness, Micah whittled away at the cover-up. He located transplanted former litigants, employees, witnesses, and experts. He obtained sworn statements from all, under penalty of perjury, that previous statements or testimony were coerced by threats or promises of significant compensation by Vincent Smith and his executive team. Micah recovered audio and video tapes of formal meetings and casual conversations detailing multiple cover-up plots across North America.

Because of Micah's stellar investigation, Blake and Kramer had Smith by the short hairs, with concrete evidence of discovery breaches, illegal payoffs, perjury, and public policy violations. At the Blake Law Offices in Bloomfield Hills, Andrea and Zack discussed strategy as the first of the bellwether cases approached.

Zack wanted to wait for trial and embarrass Smith with the evidence. Andrea correctly argued that the discovery rules required disclosure. Zack's approach was no more than a high-road version of Smith's deceptive approach.

"Seriously, Andrea? I'm withholding and springing the *truth*. Smith has lied and cheated throughout this entire litigation."

"By withholding and *not* springing the truth. The strategy you propose is almost identical. Surely, you recognize that." She wished she could speak to Michael, but he was opposing counsel.

"I'll concede your point, but my behavior is for the greater good. Smith's behavior is to conceal defects, thwart justice, and keep dangerous products on the market. Surely, *you* recognize *that*."

They bickered, agreed to disagree, and Andrea backed off. Her first duty was to the *client*, and Zack's strategy, if the case went to trial, would most likely result in higher compensation.

Michael

On the defense side, Michael was deeply troubled by what he privately called the Taggert-Smith strategy. Though retained by Smith before Taggert, Michael was not lead counsel. Thus, he contributed expertise and opinion but did participate in final decisions.

Vincent Smith and his executive team knew the company made defective and dangerous toys. Michael credited company management for pulling the toys from store shelves and replacing them with safer versions. He also knew that Smith Toys did so only when forced. As severe injuries and deaths mounted, management acted only when hiding product defects and multiple insurance claims became virtually impossible.

"Blake and Kramer are quality lawyers," Michael argued. "Serious discovery violations, illegal payoffs to witnesses, perjury, and non-disclosure agreements that are borderline bribes are not solid defense strategies. If Blake and Kramer get wind of this, we won't just lose the case, criminal penalties might apply. Lawyers could get disbarred."

Michael believed Taggert was once again setting him up to be a scapegoat. At the end of this so-called strategy, chief litigators would share most of the blame. For protection, Michael surreptitiously taped legal meetings and strategy sessions. He possessed solid evidence of unethical, even illegal, strategies and actions committed by Taggert and Smith.

Michael, however, did nothing to stop them. He was complicit. While he *argued* for full disclosure and an aggressive settlement grid, he did not go to the bar. His ethical duty required him to report all violations.

He voted against these behaviors but conceded to the majority and helped implement the strategy every time. His law practice depended heavily on the Smith Toy litigation. He decided he could not be a whistleblower because discussions between attorneys and their clients were privileged. He was in a rock-hard place situation.

Michael knew Zack Blake, but only as a worthy opponent. His relationship with Andrea was different. They shared *everything*. The case was the *only* thing they never discussed. Michael desperately wanted to share what he knew with Andrea. But he couldn't. They were on opposite sides of the case. Increasingly, Michael's ethical dilemma became a deep wedge in their relationship.

Up to that point, bedroom intimacy was no problem. In their lovemaking, they were like finely tuned instruments. Each knew what the other desired and when. They knew where and how to touch, kiss, and make their partner shiver, squirm, or gasp with pleasure. Their timing and rhythm were perfect, synchronized to increase pleasure, build to the brink, gently pull back, and increase again to a glorious climax. Recently, though, they were experiencing problems in the bedroom.

"What's wrong, Michael?"

"I'm tired."

"Tired? We're awake. I'm lying here next to you. Since when has tired stopped you?"

"Leave me alone. I can't talk about it."

"Smith Toys?"

"You know I can't answer that."

"I knew this would happen. We hardly talk to each other. I don't see you in the office. The staff separated—must we now separate from each other?"

"It won't be like this forever."

"You're my best friend. My chief confidant. We can't even *talk* about this. It's affecting our personal lives. Worse, it's affecting our intimacy," Andrea moaned.

"How the hell do you think *I* feel?" He snapped. "You're *my* best friend, too. *You're* not available to *me*. Who do *I* talk to, huh? I'm the outsider, the new guy in a strange town. You have tons of support. I have bupkis," he grumbled.

Michael worried that the relationship would not survive the Smith Toy case.

***

A bellwether trial in multi-district litigation (MDL) is, essentially, a sample trial. MDL judges hope the parties can settle their disputes during the pre-trial process. However, human nature often gets in the way, and attorneys dig in, assuming their side will win, even when the evidence suggests otherwise.

With the first bellwether trial looming, Michael was *terrified* that Andrea and Zack knew about the defense's discovery violations. As such, Michael encouraged his client and co-counsel to consider settlement or formal mediation.

Taggert and Smith opposed any offer of settlement. Stu Taggert all but promised Vince Smith that the discovery violations would reduce bellwether jury verdicts to reasonable, acceptable amounts. Why offer generous settlement terms when you will likely kick ass at trial? Under a murky cloud, Judge Kolber set the first bellwether case for trial in ninety days.

CHAPTER TWENTY-TWO

Andrea

Andrea and Zack met by Zoom conference to discuss trial strategy and work assignments. The evidence Micah compiled was overwhelming. In their original form, the toy soldiers were a choking and chemical hazard. Micah assembled considerable scientific evidence and some terrific experts to prove it.

The fact that Smith rectified the problem, removed the defective toys from store shelves, and replaced them with safer toys was not admissible evidence. By court rule, subsequent remedial measures are not admissible to prove negligence or a failure to warn the public. However, they may be admissible for other purposes, such as impeaching a witness.

Zack believed he could get the recall into evidence under at least one of the exceptions. He planned to call Smith and others to the stand. When they lied under oath, he'd impeach them with evidence that they removed defective toys and replaced them with safer toys. Andrea lobbied for full disclosure of all witnesses, which would give Smith and Taggert a heads-up about the strategy.

"It's the right thing to do, Zack. We don't want a pissed-off judge," Andrea argued.

"I know Judge Kolber. He will be more pissed at their discovery violations than at our non-disclosure of witnesses," Zack countered.

"True, but my way, Kolber slams them anyway, and we look like white knights instead of unethical attorneys who withheld evidence. We also avoid the risk that Kolber disqualifies our witnesses."

Ultimately, the great Zachary Blake reversed course and acquiesced to young Andrea Kramer's ethical disclosure strategy. Her strategy paid immediate dividends. The disclosures terrified the defense and panicked Michael O'Hara and Stu Taggert.

Michael

Taggert, Smith, and O'Hara met in the conference room at Smith headquarters.

"I warned you, Stu. They have us by the balls. I can understand underestimating Andrea Kramer, a relative newbie, but *Zack Blake*? On what planet did you not anticipate that Blake would uncover everything you failed to disclose?" Michael piled on for Smith.

"Don't get all self-righteous with me, O'Hara. You were in the room for every one of these decisions," Taggert bristled.

"And the record will reflect that I *objected* every single time. I knew this would happen. These are great lawyers. It was only a matter of time."

"Michael, what do you propose?" A terrified Vince Smith suddenly respected Michael O'Hara.

"Concede liability. Come clean. Perhaps we can still settle for a reasonable number."

"Stu?" Smith turned to Taggert.

"I agree, Vince. The non-disclosure strategy was predicated on Blake and Kramer never uncovering the evidence. Now that they have, the jig is up. It is time for us to limit damages rather than argue that there is no liability."

Smith deliberated, carefully considering his words. He continued to face Taggert.

"It strikes me, Stu, that your so-called non-disclosure strategy vastly underestimated the talents of Blake and Kramer. Would you agree?"

"That's Monday morning quarterbacking at its finest. As I recall, Vince, you *engineered* the strategy of obtaining non-disclosure agreements and court seals."

"True, but I am not a lawyer. I looked to you two for legal guidance and advice. One of you let me down. Michael's advice was spot on. I should have listened to him. I should never have added you to the team.

"Taggert, your services are no longer required. Smith Toys will press forward with O'Hara as lead counsel."

Smith turned to face Michael. "Michael, you have carte blanche to replace Taggert attorneys with competent lawyers of your choosing."

"Thanks, Vince. I appreciate the confidence and the kind words." *Finally!*

"Be reasonable, Vince. This is a harsh decision and too late in the game. Mark my words. This will have negative consequences," Stu pleaded.

"Perhaps so, but I need to stop the hemorrhaging *now*. A sound legal and *ethical* approach is needed. Michael's ethics are superior to yours."

Taggert stood, pounded the table, and addressed Smith.

"You? The guy who killed kids with his products and covered up his crimes dares to lecture *me* on legal ethics? Screw you! The two of you *deserve* each other."

Taggert glanced at Michael. O'Hara's slight smirk sent Taggert into hysterics.

"O'Hara's a lightweight!" Taggert roared. "There's a reason Taggert, Miles & Freeman dumped his sorry ass!"

"Still, I'll take my chances with Michael," Smith retorted.

Taggert huffed, glared again at a smug-looking Michael, gathered his briefcase, and stormed out of the conference room.

"The ball is now yours to run with, Michael. I trust you will advance it wisely toward the goal line. You share space with Kramer. Perhaps you can leverage that relationship?" Smith floated.

"With all due respect, Vince. Isn't that the type of thinking that put us in this predicament? I *will* approach Andrea and Zack. I won't use our relationship as a bargaining tool. I'll negotiate in good faith and get you the best outcome possible. If that's not good enough, get Taggert back in here."

Smith wisely backed off. "I apologize for the suggestion. Carry on."

CHAPTER TWENTY-THREE

Andrea

Andrea and Zack soon learned of Taggert's departure and Michael's new complete disclosure strategy.

Michael executed a full-blown document dump, but not the usual find a needle in a haystack turnover. Michael's team carefully indexed and color-coded the files. Andrea and Zack could easily locate every piece of evidence. Settlement negotiations commenced in earnest.

Judge Kolber conducted a pre-trial. Michael's full disclosure policy sharply minimized the impact of Smith Toys' and Taggert's misconduct. The judge issued an order setting forth initial procedures to select the cases for bellwether trials. Deadlines and instructions for conducting those trials were determined by court order.

At the pretrial, thirty-one-hundred-fifty cases were consolidated into the Smith Toys MDL. To participate, plaintiffs had to file their claims, state their injuries, and allege one of two causes. Was the plaintiff a choking victim or a chemical ingestion victim? A database of claimants, called a claims register, was established.

Three weeks later, Zachary Blake, Plaintiffs' Leadership Co-Counsel, submitted a list of five types of cancer they intended to litigate in the MDL. The list strictly adhered to Micah Love's investigative findings that Smith's hand-picked scientific experts opined there were reasonable links to Smith's toys and the five types of cancer: Tracheal, oral, esophageal, lung, and colorectal/intestinal.

Two months later, both parties submitted lists of plaintiffs who satisfied case eligibility criteria. The judge selected seven cases for the initial round of bellwether trials as settlement negotiations began in earnest.

After a whirlwind of activity, the parties agreed to non-binding mediation and attempted to settle the seven cases that qualified for bellwether status. Blake referred to these as 'The Magnificent Seven.' Both sides agreed to retain Michigan trial lawyer and mediator extraordinaire David Waldman, an experienced mediator who mediated and resolved numerous MDL cases during his stellar career. Judge Kolber was delighted with the facilitation news, especially with the appointment of Waldman, who rarely failed to resolve multi-district litigation.

Before the facilitation was conducted, Andrea received exciting news from the Michigan Supreme Court on the Longbow case. The justices rejected every claim of appeal and awarded additional costs to the Plaintiff. The decision prompted a last-gasp effort to resolve the litigation and end any chance of future appeals. The Taggert firm offered ninety percent of the verdict amount and no interest. Andrea rejected the offer.

Taggert recommended mediation. Andrea balked until Taggert sweetened the offer. Andrea accepted a high-low agreement. The mediator would have broad powers to select the high, low, or a number between the two. No future appeals would be filed.

The high number was the current verdict figure with interest. The low number was Taggert's last offer, ninety percent of the verdict, with no interest, a tad lower than the original jury verdict. One way or another,

Andrea would soon be a wealthy woman. She prayed Longbow would hang around long enough to see justice done and direct the best use of settlement proceeds.

The parties chose Lisa Canfield, an experienced civil rights and social justice mediator. Judge Alvin Rubin *loved* her for her perfect record of case settlements. Legal professionals praised Lisa and called her '*The Caseraser*' for her ability to drastically unclog judicial dockets.

A week before the first bellwether trial in the Smith Toys case, the Longbow case settled for fifteen million dollars, close to the high-end figure. The state of Michigan drew and tendered same-day checks at Canfield's office. A jubilant Andrea telephoned Arthur Longbow to give him the good news. A caregiver answered. Longbow was asleep and had taken a turn for the worse.

Andrea left a message requesting a return phone call. She had good news to report. The caregiver promised to deliver the message.

Andrea called Sheila.

"I've got great news!" Andrea exclaimed.

"I'm all ears."

"Longbow settled. Guess the number," Andrea challenged her.

"Seven million?"

"Higher."

"Ten?"

"Higher."

"Incredible. I give up. I can't handle the suspense."

"Fifteen Million! You've got a nice bonus coming. Start a PAC for your political campaign," Andrea joked.

"That's wonderful, Andi! You hit a frigging home run! Mr. Longbow must be extremely pleased."

"He doesn't know. He was sleeping when I called."

The following day, Andrea called Blake. He was overjoyed with the news, wishing her another *Mazel Tov*, praising her case strategy and choice of Lisa Canfield as the facilitator.

"Lisa never fails. Wise choice. How did you know about her? She's in high demand. Wouldn't typically mediate for a relative rookie, no offense."

"None taken. Micah gave me her name. She jumped in with both feet when I told her about the case. The bigger surprise was that Stu Taggert accepted her as the facilitator."

"Don't kid yourself, Andrea. Taggert knew you kicked his ass. So did the governor. They accepted Canfield because she settles cases. Did Lisa shave a million or so off the verdict? *That's* what they wanted," Zack rationalized.

"Geez, Zack. I would have done that months ago. They didn't need Canfield."

"They couldn't cave for *you*, but *everyone* caves for Canfield. There are egos involved. Get it? Plausible deniability. They'll tell the AG that Canfield stuck it to them. They had little choice but to settle."

"Pretty cynical evaluation of the facts and circumstances, wouldn't you say?"

"Cynical as hell, but it's the truth," Zack declared.

"Let them save face. You know, I know, and Taggert knows, I kicked their ass. Wait until O'Hara finds out." Andrea pictured Michael's joyful reaction.

"O'Hara has no love lost for Taggert. He should be very happy for you."

"I'm an equal opportunity ass-kicker. Michael and Smith Toys are about to experience Andreas Rectumoneous," Andrea growled.

Zack laughed out loud. "Latin for an Andrea ass-kicking? I love it! Andreas what?"

"I forgot. What did I say? Rectum something . . . Rectumoneous? Hell, I don't remember!" Now, both lawyers were in hysterics.

"You should use that in your marketing campaign. I've got to tell Jennifer that one."

"Your wife?"

"My wife. The mother of my children. The love of my life. The kingmaker. Everything I am, I owe to her."

"Wow. Someday, I hope I find a man that feels that way about me."

"Hang in there, Kramer. He's out there. You deserve that kind of happiness. I've got to run. See you at the rectum . . . uh . . . ass-kicking," he quipped. They both laughed a second time.

He's out there, Zack. Andrea's thoughts turned to Michael.

"Take care, Zack. Thanks for everything."

"You're welcome. You're one hell of a young lawyer. You have a bright future ahead of you."

"Thank you. Hopefully, Waldman will help make it so. He's a wonderful choice to facilitate this case. The Lisa Canfield of product liability cases," Andrea noted. "I agree."

"We must address the cost issue on Smith Toys as soon as the Longbow checks clear, okay?"

"Okay. Welcome to the big leagues."

CHAPTER TWENTY-FOUR

Andrea

Shortly after her conversation with Zack Blake, Andrea's cell phone rang. The caller ID read "Longbow."

"Mr. Longbow. Nice to hear from you. How are you feeling?"

"Doing a little better. I just woke up from a nice snooze. My caregiver tells me you have some news?"

"Indeed. We mediated your case and reached an agreement, pending your approval."

"What does that mean?"

"It means I can't settle the case without your permission."

"Oh . . . that makes sense, I guess. You can settle the case if that's what you want."

"How can you give me permission when you don't know the settlement amount?"

"I've learned to trust you. Besides, no amount of money will bring my Marcy back to me."

"Are you sitting down?"

"I'm lying down."

"We settled the case for fifteen million dollars."

"Holy smokes! That's higher than the verdict."

"We had court costs, file costs and expenses, appellate costs, and accrued interest for all the time they wasted in litigation. The settlement considers all that, even though it isn't everything they owe you to date."

"The settlement is much more than I anticipated. With that kind of money, I can do many good things in Marcy's name. You sure do keep your promises, young lady. Thank you so much."

Andrea could feel his spirits lifting. This financial boost might be good medicine for his ailing heart.

"I understand your health has not been good. You must get well so we can plan how you might best utilize your share of the proceeds. Perhaps we could create a charitable trust for the causes Marcy believed in. Let's get together when you are feeling better."

"Sounds good. You are an amazing lawyer and an even better person. I can't thank you enough. I feel better already. We'll talk soon."

"Thanks, Mr. Longbow. Have a wonderful day."

Michael O'Hara walked into Andrea's office as she was finishing her telephone call.

"Longbow? I heard about the settlement. Congratulations. You deserve it."

"*He* deserves it, Michael. There's no loss worse than the loss of a child. It goes against the natural order of things. Her death resulted from preventable tragedy over political nonsense. It makes my blood boil! People should be in jail."

"Perhaps. Privilege prevents me from talking much. I'm happy for you and pleased that Taggert took it on the chin again."

"Thanks. What's up?"

"Facilitation is approaching. Do you want to set some ground rules?"

"Happy to chat. I'll set up a Zoom meeting with Zack Blake and David Waldman, or we can all get some coffee somewhere and talk this over," Andrea suggested.

"Whichever. Wow!" Michael exclaimed. "Can you believe what's happened to us? From scrounging for used furniture, renting a haunted house for an office, and using lawn furniture for side chairs, to seven-figure defense fees, a nine-figure settlement, and a multi-million-dollar MDL. Isn't the law biz amazing? How about we have dinner to celebrate our good fortune?"

"After all this hard work and stress, not seeing each other socially for weeks, dinner together sounds wonderful. One hard and fast rule, however," Andrea insisted.

"What's that?"

"We will not talk business at dinner."

"Amen to that," Michael concurred. "How about Ann Arbor? *The Gandy Dancer*?"

"I *love The Gandy Dancer*. I haven't been there in ages," Andrea effused.

"It's a date, then. I took the liberty of booking us a room at *Weber's Boutique Hotel*. We can drive back to Saline in the morning. What do you say?"

"How presumptuous of you," she scoffed.

"We haven't enjoyed the personal side of our relationship in quite some time. Sorry if I jumped the gun. We've been extremely professional. I desperately *want* this evening. But I'll cancel if that's what you want," Michael offered.

"Ha! Got you!" she teased. "Turn down a fabulous evening with my favorite stud? Are you kidding me? *The Gandy Dancer* and *Weber's*? What fabulous ideas! You should be an event planner for sexually frustrated couples!"

"You sure? Blake won't mind?"

"I don't know. Would Vince Smith mind?"

"I won't tell if you don't."

Andrea put one finger to her lips to signal that they were sealed.

***

The Gandy Dancer is a beautifully restored 1886 Michigan Central Depot. The food is excellent, and the historic atmosphere is unique. It was one of Andrea's favorite places in the area. Part of the famous Chuck Muer chain of restaurants, it features seafood, Muer's signature Martha's Vineyard Salad, and Charley's Chowder, Andrea's favorite soup.

They sat in a cozy booth, having just finished placing their order. Andrea ordered the Maryland Style Crab Cakes and Michael the Parmesan Snapper and Shrimp. Andrea insisted on chowder for two.

As they waited for their soup, Michael reached across the table and took Andrea's hand. They gazed at each other wordlessly, enjoying the peacefulness of the moment, free of stress, litigation, combat, and clients on opposite sides of their cases. Michael spoke first.

"Fifteen-million-dollars! Wow! What an accomplishment! I am so proud of you."

"High praise coming from you. Thank you. As you well know, though, the case was hard to lose. The former governor's conduct was egregious. I've always felt it was only a matter of time and the amount of recovery. I never considered the possibility of losing."

"I was a sacrificial lamb. No partner had the guts to try that case. They didn't want to piss off the new administration. On a positive note, though, it brought us together."

"True. More importantly, Mr. Longbow can establish a legacy for his daughter. That's the main accomplishment and my goal in pursuing the litigation."

"You are officially a multi-millionaire. How does it feel?"

Andrea giggled. "I don't feel much different. It hasn't sunk in yet. Money has never been a motivator. I'm not knocking it but boosting Mr. Longbow's spirits is the greater achievement."

"You are something, Kramer." Michael pulled her hand up off the table and kissed her fingers.

"We still have a case to finish, Michael," Andrea cautioned.

"I thought we weren't talking business," Michael countered.

"You brought up the Longbow situation," she scolded. "I am very content not to discuss business."

"What would you like to talk about?"

"Let's talk about you. Where do you see yourself next year after the Smith case is over?" she wondered aloud.

"At the office with you."

"Doing what?"

"Loving you."

"That's a cop-out. You know what I mean."

"Not discussing business."

"I forgot. Where do you see yourself personally?"

"Loving you."

Andrea laughed. "You are a hopeless romantic. This dinner, and later, *Weber's*." She did the Groucho eyebrow waggle. "A fabulous idea; you are something else."

"I'm glad you feel that way. I wasn't sure you'd agree to come."

"Why wouldn't I?"

"I don't know. I thought that maybe, first, you'd want to finish the case. You did suggest you wanted to cool things down."

"I am happy to be here, Michael."

They fell silent. Andrea grabbed her soup spoon. Michael looked confused.

The waiter approached from behind Michael. Andrea saw the guy coming. She smelled her delicious chowder halfway across the dining room. She motioned for him to place the bowl between them and immediately scarfed down a spoonful.

"World famous," Andrea praised. She took another sip. Soup dribbled down her chin. "Mm, mm, this is outstanding."

Michael took his first sip. "This *is* delicious. What else are they famous for?"

"Wait until you taste the key lime pie. It's to die for," Andrea gushed.

The meal was fabulous. Andrea made love to a piece of key lime pie, savoring every bite. Michael sipped a cup of coffee. Andrea set down her fork and stared into space.

"What?" Michael inquired.

"Do you think working together helps or hurts our relationship?"

"There's a question out of left field! What made you ask it?"

"Never answer a question with a question, my dad used to say. What do you think?" she probed.

"I love working with you. Think about how little we would see each other if we worked in separate offices. If I'm being brutally honest, I think it has brought us closer in some ways and more distant in others."

"Distant how?"

"Our careers started on opposite sides. When Vincent Smith walked into the office, there was never a possibility you would take his case, but it was a perfect fit for me. I would say that working together, at least so far, has not been a great professional or personal fit, but it *has* been a financial windfall. Does that make sense?"

"It makes perfect sense, and I appreciate your honesty. Here's mine: I don't ever see myself representing corporate defendants. Are we forever doomed to be on opposite sides? Do you believe we have shared values?" she grimaced.

"The more Vince Smiths I meet, the more I lean toward representing worthy clients. Be patient with me. I'm still a work in progress."

"Aren't we all? I'm glad to hear you say this. Having opposite professional perspectives can't be good for our long-term future. It's a fly in the ointment, so to speak," she rationalized.

"We're talking business again," he warned.

"But only as it relates to the personal. It makes me uncomfortable to always be on opposite sides of litigation. I feel distant from you."

"I feel your pain. Me too."

"Let me ask the question another way: Ruth Bader Ginsberg or Antonin Scalia?"

"That's an interesting question with no simple answer. They liked and respected each other for a reason. I value Scalia's intellect and perspective. I envy Ginsberg's judicial conscience and passion for justice."

"Choose," she demanded, folding her arms over her chest.

"I'm not ready to make a choice," he replied.

"So, what do we do?"

"As I said, be patient. The Smith Toy case is almost over. How about we wait and see what's what?"

Her attitude changed on a dime. "What's what? Didn't you book a room at *Weber's*?" She did the eye-waggle.

"Check, please!" Michael summoned the waiter.

***

The front desk clerk at *Weber's* upgraded them to a deluxe room with a king-sized bed. The room had been recently renovated, with a large memory foam bed, modern furnishings, and a bathroom that featured amenities Andrea was not accustomed to having.

The shower featured multiple heads, a large rain head, multiple side heads, and a large wand. The toilet had a motion sensor, a lighted toilet seat, and a heated bidet. Andrea giggled when the toilet seat lit up and raised as she walked by.

"Fancy schmancy," she laughed.

Michael turned off the overhead light, and the room went immediately quiet and dark. He clicked on a lamp, turning the knob three times until the light was soft.

"Mood lighting? Andrea teased. She excused herself and walked into the bathroom. When finished, she silently cracked open the bathroom door and peeked out. Michael stood in the room. He removed his shoes, sports jacket, shirt, and slacks, neatly placing each item in the wardrobe. His bronze, chiseled body glowed in the dim light. He took down the bed and located the television clicker. He was about to turn on the television and climb into bed when the bathroom door opened.

Andrea stood at the threshold, naked, her body glistening in the dim light.

"Andrea," Michael gasped. "You're a goddess." He stood in place, looking uncertain.

She studied every inch of him. "You're not so bad yourself. Shall we?" She pointed to the bed.

Michael yanked off his boxers and sprinted to the bed. Andrea pranced to the other side, slowly, deliberately teasing him, trying to increase his desire.

"Are you alright?" she whispered as she climbed under the sheets.

"No! I'm not alright. It's been a while since the storm. You are so beautiful!"

She wanted the moment to be perfect. He kissed her, merely brushing her lips, lingering, gently probing with the tip of his tongue. She pulled him closer and leaned her arm forward toward the lamp.

"Too dark?" he asked.

"No," she replied, "too light." Suddenly, the room faded into darkness.

Later that evening, they lay together in silence.

"How do you feel?" Michael whispered.

"Wonderful, Michael. I feel . . . wonderful," she confessed with a sigh. "Do you feel it, too?"

"I do. Every moment together should mean something, especially our most intimate moments. They mean a lot to me."

"To me, as well."

"I'm pleased you feel that way . . . Want to do it again?"

***

The following morning, Michael and Andrea stepped into the bathroom. Like children, they played with all the toilet and shower gadgets, utilizing every possible nozzle variation. They made love in the shower with all conceivable shower heads pulsating above them. Andrea delighted in teasing Michael by soaping and washing his body.

After toweling off, they dressed and ate breakfast in the hotel restaurant. Both ordered the breakfast special and coffee. The waiter brought coffee and walked away to place their order.

"Last night was amazing, Andrea. This morning wasn't bad, either. I was not in a good place before I came to Saline. I mistreated a woman who loved me. I couldn't love her back. I was still reeling from the experience with Taggert."

"I feel for the lady, Michael. I do, but I also feel we were meant to be. You weren't ready. You weren't in love. Simple. It may be terrible to say, but her loss is my gain. I caught you at the right time."

"Perhaps so, but I have a confession to make."

"What's that?"

"Sarah never had a chance."

"Sarah? Her name was Sarah?"

"Yes."

Andrea raised her coffee cup. Michael followed her lead.

"To Sarah. May she soon find love with someone other than you."

"Amen."

Andrea and Michael enjoyed the rest of their breakfast in relative silence, checked out of the hotel, and headed back to Saline.

CHAPTER TWENTY-FIVE

Andrea

A ndrea and Michael returned to the office from Ann Arbor as the Smith Toy case heated up. Andrea was not lead MDL counsel, but her recent success in the Longbow litigation elevated her status.

Over the last two weeks, the parties engaged in an intense Zoom facilitation and negotiation before David Waldman, the mediator appointed by Judge Kolber. With Waldman's assistance, they established what is commonly known as a settlement grid. There were now *three* broad types of injury: choking, cancer, or a combination of both. Compensation categories were based on those types and the severity of illness or injury.

Based on the number of claims and the injury classifications, the global settlement was seven hundred fifty million dollars. Zack and Andrea weren't satisfied. They leaned on Waldman to press for punitive damages to punish Smith for his ruthless behavior, especially for concealing evidence. The more they pushed, the more frustrated Michael became.

"This is a *negotiation*, Michael argued. "You two act like it's a *crucifixion*!"

The parties finally agreed to a two hundred fifty million dollar punitive damages award. Thus, the plaintiffs were set to receive a record one billion dollars. The final puzzle piece was attorney fees. Michael argued that the large resolution *included* fees. Zack and Andrea wanted a separate award. When they couldn't agree, Waldman packed his briefcase and kicked the matter back to the trial judge. A disappointed Judge Kolber set a hearing date on the issue.

Andrea and Michael sat in the conference room of the Kramer Law Offices.

"Tough couple of weeks. We've hardly seen each other unless you count Zoom meetings," Andrea noted. She poured herself a cup of coffee.

"Coffee?" she offered Michael.

"No thanks. I've got the jitters from too much caffeine. I miss you."

"I miss you, too. It'll be over soon."

"I hope so. Blake is such a greedy bastard!" Michael fumed.

"How so?" Andrea didn't understand.

"Attorney fees? On top of a *billion* dollars? How much is enough?" he sizzled.

"I'm sorry you feel that way, Michael. I agree with Zack. Smith is a criminal. He literally and knowingly *killed* people and then tried to cover the whole thing up."

"And you negotiated an extra two hundred fifty million in punitives for his misconduct. What does that have to do with attorney fees?" Michael grumbled.

"Had he come clean in the first instance, we would have had a much easier time resolving the case. Significant hours, including investigative, were spent proving that Smith lied about the causal link between the toys and cancer. His egregious behavior resulted in significant and unnecessary investigative costs and attorney fees," Andrea reasoned.

"True, perhaps. That's why you got punitive damages! Those extra hours are covered. How much is enough? Frankly, I'm surprised you disagree. You're a reasonable person."

"I believe that Smith should pay attorney fees. Why should the plaintiffs pay lawyers for Smith's criminal misconduct? He's fortunate no one has thought to do a *criminal* investigation."

"Give me a break. Get off your social justice soapbox for a minute."

Andrea was pissed. "Don't get all high and mighty with me, O'Hara. You do not have the high road here. Not even close. Please don't lecture me about greed. Why do you suppose Smith let all those kids die?"

"All those kids? It was a handful!" he shouted.

"What if the kids were ours?"

"Ours?"

"Ours. Yours and mine. What if we were married and lost a kid or two to a Smith soldier? What if they suffered before they died?"

"That's a stretch. Leave us out of this. Quite the sympathy play," he mocked her.

"And you have no empathy! You certainly aren't ready to be a father," Andrea bristled.

"I'm in deep shit, aren't I?" Michael muttered.

"What do you think?" She stormed out of the conference room and slammed the door in his face

Fifteen minutes later, a sheet of white copy paper taped to a pencil waved through the door of Andrea Kramer's office.

"I come in peace. May I enter, Your Highness?" Michael bowed.

"You may, subject. Pay homage," Andrea played along.

"Please accept my humble apology, Your Highness. There's no harm in requesting attorney fees on a case you've won. I was out of line."

"I don't know, serf. You sounded like Taggert."

"I'm getting a shitload of heat from Smith. He believed the honest approach would save him money. The company's insurance limits won't come close to covering the final settlement. He'll go wild when I tell him the judge might add attorney fees to a ten-figure award."

"I'm sorry our motion put you in that situation, but the decision to seek attorney fees is not based on greed. My clients deserve fees, and we would be remiss if we didn't go after them."

"I understand. May I take you to dinner to make it up to you?" He waved his makeshift peace flag and pouted.

"Pull in that lower lip, peasant!" she commanded. "I am pleased to dine with you. I despise arguing over these issues. Must we keep repeating these episodes?"

"Heaven's no. This will all be over soon," he promised.

"Until the next case, we're on opposite sides," she cautioned.

"We'll cross that bridge when we get there. Onward to dinner, fair maiden." He stood with his peace pencil and pointed out the door.

"Lead the way."

Michael

With their crisis averted, Michael, Andrea, Blake, and Smith met outside Judge Kolber's courtroom.

"You do not have the high road, Vince. If you persist, Kolber will slam you on the attorney fee issue," Michael advised.

"Why?"

"The judge received the facilitator's final recommendation and proposal. He understands why there's no final settlement. He'll hold you responsible," Michael opined.

"Why me? It takes two to tango."

"True, but it takes enormous legal talent to posture a case to resolve a billion-dollar case out of court. I'm concerned he'll award an even higher fee."

Smith would have none of it. "I gambled. I lost. I've been duly punished, and I'm paying dearly. The company's insurance coverage isn't nearly enough. My company is teetering on bankruptcy. This is more salt on a painful, open wound."

"You *killed* children, Mr. Smith! Your litigation strategy was to lie and cover up, drastically increasing attorney hours. It's time to pay for that strategy," Andrea blasted him.

"Even if the judge awards attorney fees, I don't have the money. You'll jeopardize your clients' mediation award. Understood?" Smith grumbled.

"You've lied and cheated throughout. Why would anyone believe you now?" Zack asked.

"Because it's *true*! Michael, please help me out. Since you took over, haven't I traveled on the straight and narrow? Taggert recommended and strategized the bulk of the bad stuff. Surely, you've told the judge."

"He has, and we appreciate the refreshing change. But the previous behavior *permeates* this litigation. It is simply too egregious to ignore," Zack explained.

"My God, this never ends! How much more are you looking for?" Smith sighed.

"A third of a billion is over three hundred thirty-three million, but we'll settle for three hundred," Zack deadpanned.

"Three hundred what? *Million*? Are you out of your mind? The money's not there."

"Deposit more," Andrea suggested.

"Michael, you've been strangely quiet. *Defend* me!" Smith urged.

"I can't defend what you've done, Vince, but I can *negotiate* for you and argue the case to the judge. Who knows what Kolber might do? He's quite conservative. On the other hand," Michael turned to Zack and Andrea.

"A third of a billion is absurd. You know damn well that Kolber won't approve fees you can't justify by the hour," Michael challenged.

"Perhaps so, Michael, but he may award substantial fees *because* the outcome is so high, don't you agree?" Zack argued.

"Perhaps." Michael turned back to Smith. "Let's talk."

Andrea and Zack watched them argue down the corridor.

"Quite the ruse, Andrea. Brilliant of you to suggest an additional attorney fee award. Smith is right. You *are* a greedy little b-word."

"And Smith is a murderer. I'll match my values with his any day of the week. He's got the money. I know he does. I want this to *hurt*."

"But we don't want him putting the company into bankruptcy. Kolber might hit him big—we can't chance that. I say we accept whatever number they come back with." Zack opined.

"Agreed. Kolber's a wild card. I like sure things."

"I love you. Come work for the Blake firm. I'll make you a partner," Zack gushed. "How can someone so young have so much poise?"

"It's a gift," she deadpanned. Zack studied her. She burst out laughing.

"These last few months have been surreal, Zack! Poise? I spend most days afraid I'll screw something up and my clients will suffer. I've been very fortunate. Some might say this is pure luck."

"You tried a difficult case and got a nine-figure jury verdict. That's not luck, that's skill. You must be proud."

"I *am* proud but still terrified. Here they come." One set of lawyers walked up to the other.

"Well?" Andrea asked.

"We'll pay an additional fifty million in attorney fees and not a penny more. If the judge awards more, Smith Toys will file for bankruptcy protection. The whole settlement will be at risk," Michael contended.

Zack could hardly contain his glee. Andrea's ruse produced another fifty million dollars in the case.

"Not enough," Andrea responded. "We need at least a hundred million, or we see the judge. I don't buy your poverty bit."

"Come on, Andrea. Take the win," Michael pleaded.

Zack was astounded but stayed silent. *She couldn't possibly have bigger balls if she was a man!*

"Seventy-five million, final offer," Smith yelped.

"Sold!" Zack cried as Andrea opened her mouth to respond. She backed off with a sly grin.

"Let's put it on the record," Michael suggested, "before Andrea changes Zack's mind."

They walked into Judge Kolber's courtroom for a short hearing to memorialize the settlement. The Smith Toy litigation was resolved for one billion seventy-five million dollars. Andrea Kramer had done it again.

CHAPTER TWENTY-SIX

Michael

Ichael took the exit to West I-94 toward Saline. He was stunned at Andrea's hubris. He never believed Smith would pay a substantial punitive damages award. Andrea not only convinced Smith to pay punitive damages, but she also coaxed another seventy-five million in attorney fees! *What a woman!* His cell phone rang.

"Hello?" Michael answered.

"Where are you?"

"In the car, on my way back to Saline. I just received a final tongue-lashing from Vince Smith. I don't think I'll do much of his work in the future."

"Are you okay? Did I overreach? I didn't mean to embarrass you."

"I'm fine."

"You're lying. Our last argument was over this issue. I don't want it to be a festering sore. Zack invited me for a celebratory dinner and drinks, but I passed. How can I celebrate when you're feeling like crap?"

"I'm not lying, and I don't feel like crap. You did a great job. You represented your clients. This was Taggert's and Smith's fault. I'm relieved it's almost over. Parting with Smith isn't a bad thing. I made a shitload of money. When you get your share of the fees in this case, assuming we are together personally *and* professionally, we will have the financial independence to take whatever cases and clients we want. Smith is not a client I want to represent in the future."

"Wow! I like this new you."

"When we needed clients and money, taking on Smith as a client was necessary. After this MDL and Longbow, that is no longer the case. I have *you* to thank for that. You are something, Andrea, an amazing lawyer, and a more amazing person."

"Thanks, Michael. How far have you driven?"

"I'm on I-94 near Livernois."

"Turn around."

"Turn around?"

"Turn around."

"Why?"

"I want to celebrate."

"It's not appropriate. I'm the losing attorney. We'll look like we're in cahoots."

"Who's going to see us? Who's going to know us?"

"Where are we going?" Michael wondered.

"*Casino Hotel Windsor.*"

"Canada?"

"Why not? Good exchange rate, nice ambiance."

"I'm game," he decided.

"Good. No strip clubs, O'Hara."

"I wouldn't dream of it. Besides, I'll be with the most beautiful woman in Ontario. Everyone, male or female, will envy me."

"Aw, shucks. First, we'll gamble, then we'll each do our own little strip club act in our hotel room."

"Kramer? I like the way you think. Turning around, *now*."

Michael pulled up to the courthouse parking lot. Andrea waited for him at the front entrance. They took his car and left hers overnight in the courthouse parking lot. Michael made a Michigan left and headed for the Windsor Tunnel.

Traffic was light. Windsor was just across the Detroit River. A quick mile-long trip through the tunnel under the river, a brief discussion with a customs agent about their destination, and they pulled up to the opulent casino and hotel on Riverside Drive East. Detroit is unique—drive a mile, and you're in a different *country*.

Andrea sauntered into the casino while Michael booked a room at the hotel. "I'll meet you on the casino floor. I'm feeling lucky tonight," she called back to him.

"I thought you wanted to *get* lucky?" Michael quipped.

She turned to face him, walking backward. "The night is young." She did the Groucho Marx eyebrow thing. Michael loved her for it.

Andrea

Andrea looked around the large room and located the roulette wheel. She purchased a large stack of pink wheel chips and approached the table. Standing back awhile, she watched the players, hoping for strategic tips.

This chameleon approach worked for here in the past.

In Roulette, as with most games of pure chance, the odds favor the house—whether a player experiences a hot streak, loses every spin, or places their first bet, the odds remain the same. Andrea, though, like most chameleons, believed none of that. She did not subscribe to common sense or statistical reasoning. She sought to imitate the guy with the hot hand.

She homed in on her target, an older, heavy-set man with greasy white hair. An unlit cigar hung from his lips, and a hot young woman wearing too much make-up clung to his arm. He placed the bets. She cheered wildly, watching the wheel go around. She joyfully planted a wet kiss on his lips every time he won. And he was winning, calling the woman his good luck charm, a term she readily embraced.

After the man spread a few chips around the table, Andrea walked up and placed a few chips on top of his. The man looked up at the beautiful newcomer, studied her head to toe, and nodded. Andrea flirted back. The man's made-up companion noticed the exchange, wiggled over, and planted herself firmly between the two players, giving Andrea the stink eye.

As the croupier spun, Michael approached the table, jingling the room key. Andrea held up her hold-on finger. She grabbed his arm and pulled him to the table without taking her eyes off the wheel.

When the pill landed, Andrea and the older guy won big. Everyone cheered. The man got his kiss. So did Michael, a wet one planted firmly on the lips. Andrea was more excited about winning a few hundred at the roulette table than winning multiple millions in court.

"It's a couple hundred bucks, Andi. Think about what you won in court today."

"Don't pout, Michael. The night is young. There's more than one way to get lucky. Be patient—you'll get your turn."

"You sure know how to enjoy yourself. I'll give you that. You're a hell of a mind reader, too. What am I thinking right now?"

"Do you have the room key?"

Michael held up the key.

"You're thinking: How do I get her off this floor and up to the room?"

"Clairvoyance is another one of your many talents."

"I won't be long, besides—"

"I know, the night is young."

"Exactly. Now follow my lead."

They played roulette together, lost some of Andrea's winnings, and moved on to blackjack, Michael's game. Andrea played along but did not seem enthusiastic. She didn't like card games.

"Everyone is so serious. No one ever looks happy." She confided that she preferred roulette or the ultimate gambling high, craps.

Michael and Andrea sat at the blackjack table, nodded at the two players already present, and greeted the dealer. Michael placed initial bets in their betting boxes. The dealer dealt two up cards to each player. Michael had a queen and a nine, and Andrea a pure blackjack. The dealer had an up-card king. What was the down card? Andrea shouted with glee as the dealer uncovered an eight. The dealer declared, "We have a winner," and doubled Andrea and Michael's stacks.

They continued to play and win. Andrea was euphoric and anxious to play. However, as they played on, Andrea yawned a few times, pulled on Michael's sleeve, and signaled it was time to go upstairs. They won a final hand, tipped the dealer, and left the table.

As they walked across the casino floor, they encountered several slot machines.

Andrea stopped and asked Michael, "Get me some quarters, please?" He shrugged, rolled his eyes, and obeyed—no sense jumping before a moving train.

Armed with a stack of quarters, a rejuvenated Andrea carefully studied the machines. Most gamblers know there is no such thing as a winning slot machine. They are one hundred percent luck. There is no strategy to employ, but, according to Andrea, there were tricks and secrets to ensure a better chance of winning. Her choice of machines belied her words, as she chose the progressive slot, the machine with the longest odds and largest payouts.

"High risk, high reward," she chirped. "I've been watching this machine—lots of players, no big jackpots. It's a loose machine. I know it is. It's just waiting for someone to get lucky."

"Right," Michael grunted. "Not me, not tonight."

"You're pouting," she observed.

"I'd like to get up to the room and ravish you."

"The night—"

"Yeah, yeah, it's young," he growled.

"Party pooper."

"Can we get on with it, please?"

"Okay, Mister Grouchy."

Andrea dropped a couple of coins into the slot and pulled the lever. She lost. She repeated the act several times and continued to lose. Michael grumbled. She noticed he was growing impatient, but she couldn't stop herself. She won a few times, but her losses far outweighed her wins. The quarter stack continued to dwindle. Michael kept checking his watch. They'd been playing slots for a half-hour.

Down to her final ten quarters, and seeing that Michael was frustrated, she dropped the last ten coins into the slot and pulled the lever. It wasn't the first ten bucks she ever wasted.

They watched the slots spin. Consecutively, every slot landed on cherries. The machine lit up and continued to emit flashing lights. A loud siren sounded, turning heads at the slots. A dollar amount of twenty thousand flashed on the screen. Andrea Kramer won twenty grand on ten dollars' worth of quarters.

Other gamblers cheered and applauded. Andrea jumped for joy. Even Michael seemed excited until he learned this was a taxable jackpot and paperwork was required. The floor manager and slot attendant approached and congratulated Andrea. The same floor manager verified the jackpot.

Andrea followed them to a counter where they requested a government-issued I.D. card—she provided her driver's license—and completed paperwork for her signature. When the paperwork was completed, they handed it to the cashier. She tendered a copy of Andrea's signed document and two stacks of cash in ten-thousand-dollar bundle bands.

"We're rich!" she shrieked, forgetting about her hard-earned law practice millions in the euphoria of her gambling success. After generously tipping the slot attendant, she and Michael left the casino.

When they finally got to the room, Andrea pulled the bundle bands off the money and threw both bundles in the air. Money flew all over the room. Andrea laughed hysterically. "Just like in the movies," she shouted with glee.

Michael stood by the door. Arms folded, he smiled and watched the happy scene unfold. Andrea ran to him and jumped into his arms.

"What a night!" she cried.

"What a day!" he corrected. "Or did you forget that you and Zack coaxed another seventy-five million out of Smith?"

"That was work. This was luck! And lots of fun. You're a party pooper."

"Congratulations. What would you like to do? Room service?"

Andrea kissed him hard on the lips. "Is there a Jacuzzi tub?" She did the Groucho eye-waggle.

***

Andrea walked to the bathroom. She turned on the hot and cold water, tested the jets, and fiddled with the temperature. Satisfied, she pulled out her cell phone and mumbled, "Hey, Siri." The phone lit up, and Siri responded: "Uh-huh?" Andrea requested "love-making music." Siri chose *Love Song Radio*. Andrea turned to Michael and began removing her clothes to the music.

"Just like *Jason's*," she moaned, miming the famous strip club performers.

"Much better than *Jason's*," Michael encouraged, fumbling with the buttons on his shirt.

"What would you like to do with me?" She continued to dance and flirt.

"I haven't decided yet. What would you like me to do?" He continued to fumble with his shirt buttons.

"You are one fine specimen of a man." She felt intoxicated but could not remember taking a drink.

"Back at you," he replied.

"I'm one fine specimen of a man?" she laughed.

Michael chuckled. "You know what I mean. You are the most stunning, sexy, beautiful, and talented woman I have ever met. A gift from God."

His words touched her. "What a sweet thing to say!" She continued to strip to the music, down to her thong and bra. They locked eyes as she danced in the dim lights.

"I speak the truth, the whole truth, and nothing but the truth," he replied.

She wanted him—there and then in that jacuzzi tub. He kissed her. She felt pleasure from this simple gesture. She teased him and pushed him away, walked back to the tub, unhooked her bra, and tossed it to the floor.

Michael ripped off his shirt and threw it to the floor. He began to fumble with his belt buckle.

Andrea enjoyed teasing him. She pulled on the bands of her thong, swayed her hips, and slowly slid the panties down. Michael finally unhooked his belt and fumbled with his zipper until his trousers dropped to the floor.

Andrea danced in the nude. Michael rushed to her, but she fended him off, turned to check the water, and dumped liquid soap into the Jacuzzi. The liquid began to bubble as she turned back to Michael, took him by the hand, and led him into the tub. Andrea watched in the full-length mirror as they descended into the warm water and sank lower into the suds. Suds splashed all around them until a cozy warmth enveloped her body and took her breath away—

Later that evening, Andrea closed her eyes, feigning exhaustion. She felt Michael gently toweling her dry, a lovely gesture. When he reached her hand, she grabbed the end of the towel and moaned: "I want more."

When they finally got in bed for the night, Andrea cuddled close.

"I never knew it could be like this. I may be falling in love with you."

"Ditto," he replied, repeating the Swayze line.

"Ditto?" She chastised him.

"I may be falling in love with you, too."

They held each other close and soon fell asleep.

Michael and Andrea checked out of the hotel the following morning and drove back through the tunnel to Detroit. They stopped at the courthouse to pick up Andrea's car. Michael pulled up in front of the building, exited, and ran over to the other side to open the door for his lady.

"Chauvinist," she uttered with a smile.

"Forever. My mother taught me well."

"She did. See you at the office?"

"I'll wait here until you come out of the garage. We can follow each other to Saline."

"That's not necessary. We're not some old married couple," she joked.

"The M word?"

"Do you want me for my money or my body?"

"I just . . . want you."

"Michael?"

"Yes?"

"You're double parked. Let's discuss it at the office. Hit the road."

"You sure know how to kill a mood. Okay, but I'm holding you to it," he warned.

"I know you will." She turned her back to him and started towards the garage. He could not see the troubled look on her face. *Marriage might ruin a perfect relationship.*

CHAPTER TWENTY-SEVEN

Andrea

Michael drove off, and Andrea headed for the municipal parking garage. She immediately noticed a man in a Ford Explorer watching her from a nearby parking spot. She reached into her purse, pulled out her compact, and manipulated the mirror so that she could see the guy from behind.

He looked familiar, but she couldn't place him. He wore combat fatigues and a Detroit Lions cap. She immediately presumed that he was connected to the people involved in the insurrection at the State Capitol. *How did he know I would be here this morning?*

She decided he had followed her to the parking garage the previous night. Simple logic dictated that she'd eventually return to pick up her car. *Why? What could be so important that he would wait overnight while I was in Windsor?*

Andrea continued toward the parking garage, simultaneously watching the faux military man with her compact. The man looked both ways, jogged across Jefferson Avenue, and continued to follow her to the parking garage. Andrea thought about calling 9-1-1 but decided to let the situation play itself out. The military guy twirled three hundred sixty degrees, apparently looking for cameras. Andrea had already determined that there were none.

Andrea picked up the pace and jogged to the elevators. The man tried to keep up. He rounded the corner and stepped into the garage. Andrea entered the elevators and pressed the up button. The military guy raced to the elevator bank, attempting to stop Andrea's elevator before the doors closed.

Andre caught a glimpse of the guy immediately before the elevator doors closed in his face. *Asshole will have to wait for the next car.* She arrived on the third floor and walked toward her car. Still watching her ass with the compact mirror, she observed the guy run out of an open staircase, look around, and spot her walking away. He continued to follow.

Andrea reached back into her purse and pulled out her keychain, keys, and attachments. She opened her compact. The guy now fast-walked, getting closer and closer to Andrea. *Dumb, Kramer. You should have called the police.*

Andrea hit the remote, and her car chirped a few steps away. The man edged closer as Andrea fumbled with her keychain. He reached her as she reached her car and stuck what Andrea presumed to be a weapon in her back.

"Turn around, lady!"

She turned and shot the guy in the face with her mace-pepper spray keychain. Military man, in agony, dropped his gun. He placed both hands in front of his eyes.

"What the hell?" he cried.

Andrea picked up the gun and pointed it at North.

"Who the hell are you? I know you can't see me, but I have your gun. It's pointed at your face, and I am calling the cops. I don't see any cameras, do you? Silly question, of *course* you don't!

"I can tell the police any story I want. You tried to abduct me at gunpoint, I shot you in the face with pepper spray, we struggled for the gun, and it went off. I was defending myself, officer. I didn't mean to *kill* him. capiche?"

"Yes."

"Good, now talk while you still can."

"Screw you!" North tried defiance.

"Suit yourself." Andrea pulled back the trigger. It made a distinctive clicking sound.

"Wait, wait, okay! You win. What do you want to know?"

"Who are you, and why are you trying to abduct me? That is what you are doing, correct? Trying to abduct me?"

"Yes. My name is Brandon North. I'm a member of the Michigan Watch Patrol."

"I'm familiar with you and your alt-right garbage. What's that have to do with me?"

"We were at the Capitol for Rinke's speech. Our members organized the Stop the Steal, Rinke for Governor rally."

"I repeat, what does that have to do with me?"

"Michigan is divided. Our people wanted Rinke reelected. Election officials declared Page the winner. We were pissed! The election was rigged!"

"Blah, blah, blah—we're not going to relitigate your crackpot election denier bullshit. One last time. What does any of this nonsense have to do with me?" As she clicked the gun trigger again, her phone chirped.

"Hang on a second, asshole. It's 9-1-1 on the line."

Andrea held her phone in one hand and pointed the gun at North with the other. "Yes, operator, my name is Andrea Kramer. I'm on the third floor of the municipal lot at Jefferson and Griswold in Detroit, across from the City-County Building. I've been abducted at gunpoint. I have managed to take the gun from the perpetrator, but he may attack again. Please send the cavalry to the coordinates shown on my cell phone."

"Come on, lady. We don't need the cops. We can work this out. I'll talk," North pleaded.

"You promise? If I call them off, you'll tell me everything?"

"Yes."

"Deal." Andrea terminated the call and spoke into a dead receiver. "Operator? Never mind. The threat has been neutralized. I can handle things on my own. No need to send officers over here."

She turned to North, still in agony, trying to open and focus his eyes. "I'm turning off my phone." She hit the record button. "Talk, or I'll call them back."

"I told you. I am Brandon North. I'm a founding member of the Michigan Watch Patrol."

"Yes, you told me. Stop stalling. Why did you try to abduct me?"

"Kidnap the lady who just won a multi-million-dollar verdict? The lady who embarrassed Gordon Rinke and forced him into hiding? Why would anyone want to do that? Maybe it was dangerous, but sacrifices are necessary to secure a brighter future and a new path for America."

"Has anyone ever told you you're a jackass? Keep talking," Andrea ordered.

"Rinke took off. No one's heard from him. Kidnap the person who single-handedly tried to put all of us in prison? Ask for a huge ransom from that tall guy who took you to Canada? Why would any of us want to do that?"

"How do you know we were in Canada?"

"We've been *watching* you, trying to catch you alone. We *followed* you."

"You followed us to Canada? You've got some balls! You're lucky Michael didn't see you. I'm *much* nicer than he is."

"That's good, I guess."

"So, *that's* what this is about—I embarrassed Gordon Rinke? That idiot embarrassed himself. Some leader!" She scoffed. "Why would you follow a coward like Rinke? When you stormed the Capitol, where was Rinke? Hiding somewhere, watching on television. He wouldn't get *his* hands dirty or jeopardize *his* life. Folks like you do his dirty work. You scumbags *killed* a wonderful young lady."

"I had nothing to do with that!"

"Did you storm the Capitol that day?"

"Yes."

"Were you in the group of men and women who came through the back? Or the group who charged up the front steps?"

"We were in the front."

"The people who charged up the front steps trampled my client, Marcy Longbow, to death. Her wonderful father will never see his daughter again. And you're responsible.

It was you and your insurrectionist comrades who trampled her to death. Admit it."

"I saw guys running over a girl, but it wasn't me."

"You *saw* her get trampled?"

"Yes. I was right there."

"Who did it?"

"If I tell you, you'll get me some kind of . . . what's it called . . . immunity?"

"I'm not a prosecutor. The cops aren't here. This is a private conversation between you and me. Attorney-client privilege might attach. Have you got any money on you?"

"No, I put it all in the parking meter. Why do you need money?"

"If you give me money and we agree I'm your lawyer, I can't talk to the police. Attorney-client privilege would attach."

"I've got no money on me. Would a promise to give you money do the trick?" North calmed. Andrea heard the faint sound of police sirens.

"I'm afraid not. There must be an exchange of consideration."

"What's that?"

"Money. Something of value."

"Information has value. I'll give you information," North promised.

"That might work. I guess it depends on the value of the information and what I'm allowed to do with it."

"I'll give you the names of the guys who killed the girl. You can do what you want, so long as I'm not charged, and the guys don't know I squealed."

"You didn't stomp on Marcy. Why would you be charged?"

"Because I've been hiding them at my headquarters in Howell."

"That's obstruction of justice. You can go to prison for that. You're a smart guy, protecting yourself like this."

"I went to community college for two semesters," North boasted. "I've raised a shitload of money for the cause."

"*That's* why you're smarter than your comrades," Andrea snickered. "Who are these guys? Telling me will go a long way to helping you out of this mess. You abducted me at gunpoint, right?"

"Yes," he admitted.

"And you charged into the Capitol the day they stampeded over Marcy Longbow?"

"I was there, but I didn't stomp on her," he waffled.

"No, you just hid the guys who stomped on her?"

"Yes," another admission.

"And their names?"

"Luther Madden, Bill Kreuger, and Neal Donovan."

"And where are those guys now?"

"At my place in Howell, hiding out."

"What's the address?"

"6220 Bainsbridge Street."

"Feel better?" Andrea asked.

"Not much."

"Not your eyes, moron, your guilty conscience—feel better for having spilled the beans?"

"I didn't spill the beans. This is a private, confidential conversation, right?"

The police sirens became louder and then stopped. Footsteps pounded up the staircase.

"What the hell? I thought the cops weren't coming. That's what you said."

"I lied. How are your eyes?"

"I still can't open them."

"Too bad. Maybe the cops will give you eye wash when they take you into custody."

"Custody? What happened to immunity?" He groaned, eyes burning.

"I decided not to take you on as a client. And I already told you. I don't work for the prosecutor or the cops. I can't grant you immunity."

"I'm not squealing to the cops." His head darted around to the sound of her voice. He squinted and averted his eyes to where he thought she would be.

"They'll get nothing out of me. You think you're so smart. They won't catch my guys. I won't talk."

"The cops won't need you to talk. Have a listen." Andrea stopped recording and hit rewind. The phone repeated North's confession.

"And where are those guys now?" The recording repeated.

"At my place in Howell, hiding out."

Andrea paused the recording.

A group of Detroit cops approached Andrea and North.

"Lower your weapon," a tall African American police sergeant ordered. Andrea complied.

"Are you the lady who called 9-1-1?"

"I am."

"Would you mind giving me the gun?"

"Not at all. It's his, not mine." Andrea gestured to North as she handed over the gun.

"How did you disarm him?"

"I shot a can of pepper spray in his face. He dropped the gun."

"He could have shot you. That was not very bright."

"It *was* dumb now that you mention it. I acted on impulse. He followed me and tried to enter the elevator, but the doors closed. My friends tell me I'm impulsive. But I couldn't let him kidnap me. It's not in my DNA," Andrea advised.

"I understand. I know women like you. One of them was my ex-wife."

"Why, ex?"

"Because she kept pulling shit like you pulled this morning."

"Sorry. Didn't mean to dig up unpleasant memories."

"Where's the pepper spray?"

Andrea reached into her purse. "It's right here." She pulled out the canister and pointed it at the sergeant.

"Hey! Get that out of my face!" the sergeant grumbled.

Andrea pointed it downward. "Sorry. Not to worry, it's empty." She pressed on the nozzle, and pepper spray harmlessly shot out, away from the officers.

"Empty? Right. The canister, please?" the sergeant huffed.

Andrea surrendered it. "Sorry, sir, I honestly thought it was empty. Do you have a name?"

"Sergeant Isaiah Brighton. You?"

"I'm a lawyer. Andrea Kramer. Nice to meet you."

"The Saline lady?"

"Yes."

"Handled the Longbow case? You're famous, Andrea. May I call you Andrea?"

"Sure. I'll call you . . . uh . . . Sergeant."

"Works for me. Who's this guy?"

"You are going to *love* me, Sergeant."

"I've already grown quite fond of you," he joked. "Why am I going to love you?"

"This guy is Brandon North."

"Why is that name familiar to me?"

"Founding member of the Michigan Watch Patrol. One of the people who planned the Capitol insurrection."

"Got it! That's why it sounded familiar. What's he got to do with you?"

"He didn't like how I embarrassed our former governor."

"That's a lame reason to abduct someone at gunpoint." He looked at North with disdain. The suspect still could not see a thing.

"I told him the same thing. There were fifteen million other reasons."

"Huh?" Sergeant Brighton didn't understand.

"The award in the Longbow case. North thought he could get my partner to pay him a ransom."

"This gets better and better," Brighton smiled.

"There's more."

"More? Keep going. You're on a roll."

"Hey! What happened to attorney-client privilege?" North interrupted. He looked terrified.

"I told you, Brandon. I decided not to take your case," Andrea scoffed. Brighton looked confused.

"Sergeant, my new friend, Brandon, has been hiding the people who trampled Marcy Longbow to death. I now know, and you will soon know the identities of these murderers."

"Oh my God! I *do* love you! How is it you know this?"

"My friend Brandon confessed to everything."

"But I ain't talking!" North yelped.

"Doesn't matter, asshole. You already talked. Listen to this." Andrea played the entire recording for the police.

"Holy shit!" Brighton turned to one of his officers. "Hainsworth, get a hold of a homicide detective! Get this recording bagged, tagged, and duplicated. Have the detective alert Howell Police and secure an arrest warrant for Madden, Donovan, and Kreuger. Give them this address." He handed Hainsworth a slip of paper.

"Sir, yes, sir." The officer hurried away. Brighton's expression changed to one of concern.

"I never asked you, Andrea. This has probably been a very traumatic experience. How are you doing? Are you okay?"

"Yes. Why wouldn't I be?"

"In my experience, most women abducted at gunpoint are *not* okay."

"I'm not most women. But thanks for asking. Do you need anything more from me?"

"Yes. Can we go to headquarters and get your formal statement? I need to log the recording into evidence and maintain strict chain of custody protocol."

"I have a busy day. Do I have a choice?"

"Not really."

"Leave my car and go with you, or take it and follow you?"

"I'd prefer you went with me."

"I need to call the office."

"You can call them from the station or on my cell."

"Thanks. Let's go."

Brighton drove Andrea to 1300 Beaubien. Andrea called the office to let them know she'd be late. Police fingerprinted and photographed Brandon North. When finished, they placed him in lock-up.

Andrea provided a written and recorded statement but was dismayed to discover that her phone was now evidence. The Detroit cops would be keeping it for a while.

"We'll get it cloned and put the data in a burner," Brighton promised. "I'll have an officer drop that off for you in Saline. Okay?"

"Do I have a choice?"

"No."

"Okay, then, I guess."

"You're a pistol," Brighton marveled.

"I've been called worse."

"Ready to go back for your car?"

"I was ready two hours ago," she quipped.

"Sorry about that. This is important. I had to do it by the book."

"I completely understand. I want these murderers behind bars."

"About that. Howell police raided the Bainsbridge Street address and arrested Madden, Kreuger, and Donovan. They'll be transported to Lansing and arraigned. The officers found a treasure trove of incriminating evidence against those three and your boy, North."

"My boy?" Andrea scoffed.

"Just an expression."

"Kidding. Keeps you on your toes," Andrea chuckled.

"You are a pistol."

"So, I've been told."

CHAPTER TWENTY-EIGHT

Michael

Michael drove southwest on I-94, casually glancing at other cars, half expecting to see Andrea pull up beside him. He thought about calling her, but she'd chastise him for being over-protective.

He drove about forty-five miles to the Saline exit and parked his car at the office a few minutes later. After exiting the vehicle, he walked through the front door.

When he entered the reception area, all hell broke loose.

"Michael, is she alright? Are you okay? Where's Andi?"

A huge congratulatory banner hung from the rafters. A long, cloth-covered table featured a tray of breakfast items and desserts from a local deli and coffee shop. The staff planned a celebration.

"What are you carrying on about? What's going on?"

"Weren't you with her this morning?"

"With who? Andrea? Yes, I was with her this morning. What the hell is going on? Someone tell me right now!" he demanded.

"She called from a *police car,* Michael! She was abducted at gunpoint!" Deb advised.

"When? Where? How is she? How did she sound?" Michael was horrified.

"I don't know, *determined,* maybe? She sounded okay on the phone. She said she'd be in later."

"Does she have her phone? I'll call her."

"No. Her phone is being kept as evidence. She can't take calls."

"Evidence? Why?"

"I'm not sure."

"I'm calling police headquarters. I've got some friends there from my time in Detroit." He looked around the lobby.

"What's all this?"

"We planned a surprise to celebrate Andrea's big win," a paralegal replied.

Michael knew Andrea would be deeply touched. Employees from both sides of the case participated in the surprise, a circumstance not overlooked by Michael.

"I'll participate. Although my side lost, I still got paid," Michael quipped. "I'm sure she'll be here soon. Let's leave all this in place and celebrate when she arrives. Thanks, guys. I know she'll appreciate this. The place looks beautiful."

The staff breathed a collective sigh of relief. They neglected to consider *Michael's* feelings about his loss and were relieved he was on board with the celebration.

Michael went into his office and called the police. His call was routed to Sergeant Isiah Brighton, the man in charge of the investigation.

Brighton didn't know Michael but knew of him. Taggert's office represented the Detroit Police. Michael and other Taggert lawyers defended numerous police misconduct cases.

Brighton filled Michael in on the circumstances of Andrea's abduction and the arrests of the four men responsible for Marcy Longbow's death. Michael listened but grew impatient waiting for Brighton to update him on Andrea's condition. Brighton continued to talk about the abduction. Michael interrupted him.

"I'm glad you caught these guys, Sergeant Brighton, but I'm more concerned with my partner. What's her condition? Where is she? Is she hurt?"

"Sorry. I thought you knew. She's fine. That woman is something else. A man pulls a gun on her, and she sprays him with mace, disarms him, and forces him to confess at gunpoint. Who does that? She's a pistol, that one. I just dropped her off at the parking garage. A squad car is following her to Saline. We've notified local police, who will maintain surveillance in case any rogue Watch Patrol guys are tailing her."

"That's my Andi," Michael sighed. "She's the last person I'd abduct at gunpoint. The guy's lucky to be alive! A pistol? You have no idea!"

"I gather she's important to you?"

"Indeed."

"You've got yourself a good one, young man. Convince her to tone down her impulsiveness and let the professionals deal with the bad guys. She can obtain justice in the courts. Next time, things might not turn out so well."

"Truer words have not been spoken. But how do you stop a human tornado?"

"That's your problem. I'll leave her in your hands. Of course, she'll have to testify at Brandon North's trial."

"Thanks for everything, Sergeant. I appreciate it."

"You're welcome, but I didn't do anything. I responded to a 9-1-1 call. When I got to the scene, your lady friend had the drop on the perp. That was a first for me. Keep an eye on her."

"I'll try. It's not easy."

"You're a lucky guy."

"I know."

They terminated the call. Michael left his office and returned to the bullpen.

"Attention, everyone. I just got off the phone with Detroit P.D. Andrea is fine—not a scratch on her. She's returning to the office with a police escort."

"Should we cancel the surprise?"

"No, after what she went through this morning, I think she'll enjoy it."

He picked up a kazoo and began to blow on it, making lots of noise, while his staff breathed a sigh of relief that the boss was safe.

A half-hour later, the receptionist announced that Andrea was in the parking lot. She was out of her car, talking to a Detroit police officer in a squad car.

"Places, everyone!" Deb shouted.

"I hope Vince Smith doesn't walk in," Michael kibitzed.

The employees paused. Was he serious? Michael blew the kazoo and shouted, "Carry on! Mimosa for everyone except me!"

Andrea walked through the door. The staff stood, yelled "surprise," and blew on kazoos.

Michael could see the gesture cheered her. She was still slightly rattled from the abduction fiasco. He wondered if she was in a mild state of shock.

The party continued through the morning. Everyone had a good time, but it was a workday. While the lawyers did not have court that morning, there were MDL clients to notify, case resolution paperwork to prepare and file with the court, and arrangements for payment to coordinate with the Blake Law Office.

Michael had to facilitate and ensure prompt paperwork and payment from Smith Toys to finalize the MDL.

As the staff retreated to their stations and lawyers to their offices or cubicles, Andrea and Michael returned to their offices.

"I feel awful, Andrea. I should have waited for you to pull out of the garage. I left you there, all alone. How are you? Please tell me you're okay. Did that bastard hurt you?"

"I'm fine, Michael. Looking back on things, I guess I'm a bit shaken. But I'm fine. As for you leaving the municipal garage, I'm *always* at the Wayne County Courthouse. I park in that lot whenever I have a case in Wayne Circuit. I'm constantly alone. What could you have done, anyway?"

"I don't know. I would have been there for you. For support, I guess. Instead, I left you alone to deal with a deranged predator."

"Get over yourself, O'Hara. This is my trauma, not yours. Who had the worst day? You or me?"

"You."

"Spoil me. Pamper me. Redirect all my office responsibilities to your office. I plan to sit here all day, relax, and maybe nap. Will you cover for me?"

"Absolutely."

"And one more thing."

"What's that?"

"Stop with the guilt. You couldn't have known. We both would have been in danger. Okay?"

"Yes, dear."

"That's better. Will you take care of the office? I'm going to lie down on this very comfortable old couch."

"I'll make sure you're not disturbed."

Michael walked over and tightly hugged her. He pushed back to face her, kissed her softly, and hugged her again. He lingered, staring down at her. *What if something had happened to you?*

Andi interrupted his thoughts. "Get out of here and do what you promised. I will not have the staff speculating about afternoon delights. Their minds are already in the gutter about our relationship."

Andrea

Michael left. Andrea entered her private bathroom. She did her business, washed her hands, and stared at herself in the mirror. *No worse for wear. You'd never know you were abducted at gunpoint this morning. How do you feel?* "Numb," she answered herself out loud.

She took her makeup out of her purse, did some touch-up work, and sighed. *I've got to call Mr. Longbow.* Andrea forgot all about her plan to rest on the couch.

She telephoned Longbow and gave him the good news.

"Mr. Longbow? This is Andrea Kramer."

"Nice to hear from you, Andrea. How are you?"

"I'm fine, sir. I have great news for you."

"More news? You are the gift that keeps on giving. What's the news?"

"The police have arrested four men who stormed the Capitol. Three of those were the men who trampled your daughter. The other planned the rally. We have them dead to rights."

Longbow gasped and then sobbed. Andrea waited until he calmed. The receiver was silent.

"Mr. Longbow? Are you okay?"

"I'm better than okay, Andrea. How do you know all this?"

"I was . . .er . . . involved in the arrest."

"This I have to hear!" Longbow laughed.

Andrea spent the next several minutes retelling the story to Arthur Longbow. She felt his spirits lifting as she spoke. When she finished, Longbow said nothing. She heard him breathing on the other end of the line.

"Mr. Longbow?"

"The best thing I've ever done, aside from marrying my wonderful wife and fathering Marcy, was walk into your office. I can never replace my wife or daughter, but you have brought me peace and justice I never thought possible. Thank you for everything you've done. God bless you."

Tears welled in Andrea's eyes. His words made her proud, but more importantly, she was focused on her client. *I brought him peace and justice.* They continued to chat about the coming arraignment and that Longbow might be needed to testify. Andrea promised to be with him every step of the way. They finished the call, said goodbye, and Andrea hung up the receiver. *I hope I lifted his spirits. He did wonders for mine!*

Shifting gears to the Smith Toys case, she called Zack Blake's office to discuss protocol for settlement distribution, fee approval and splits, and every other detail involved in resolving a significant MDL. She decided not to tell Zack about her harrowing morning.

Zack, as he was prone to do, offered to assume the burden—the experienced old hand of the group. Andrea declined, assenting to him taking the lead but requesting to be involved at every phase. "How else will I learn?" Blake agreed.

"Would you like to coordinate things with Michael, or should I?" Zack inquired.

"You do it, Zack, if you don't mind. I'm not sure where his head is. He seems happy for me, but we share space. His client is quite displeased with this outcome. I don't want to create more discomfort or rub it in his face," Andrea reasoned.

"I understand and agree," Zack assented. "Happy to coordinate protocol. Your Iolta account or mine?" Iolta accounts were the Michigan State Bar's preferred trust accounts for the deposit of client funds.

"Yours is fine, Zack. After the full accounting, we'll transfer my fees, costs, and my clients' shares."

"Okay, Andrea. Nice work yesterday. You made seventy-five million appear by magic. I didn't have the cajones to ask for more money."

"All evidence to the contrary. How does one who lacks hubris become King?

"Point taken. Still, I was satisfied with the facilitation award and the punitives. I'll remember the seventy-five-mil come fee-splitting time."

"From the bottom of my heart, thanks for inviting me to the party. I learned a lot," Andrea replied.

"As I have stated repeatedly, you *earned* your seat at the table. Stellar performance—nice work! I'll contact you when the closing documents and payment are ready."

"Thank you, kind sir."

"You're welcome."

Zack promised to keep her in the loop on everything related to the final resolution details and then terminated the call. Andrea rose and walked over to Michael's office. His door was closed. He was on the telephone. Without knocking, Andrea opened the door and sat down.

"I understand it's a lot of money, Vince. But this is the settlement *you* agreed to, not a verdict shoved down your throat by a runaway jury. The judge will expect you to step up immediately. Otherwise, expect him to penalize you," Michael warned.

Andrea suddenly realized this was a confidential conversation. She backed out of the office and returned to her own. A few minutes later, Michael knocked on her office door.

"Come in." Michael walked through the door. Andrea motioned for him to sit in one of the side chairs.

"I'm sorry if I ignored you," he began.

"No, Michael. I'm sorry for not respecting boundaries. The conversation you were having with Smith was privileged. I had no business walking in without knocking. I apologize."

"How could you know I was talking to Smith? There's no need to apologize. No harm done anyway. You already knew he'd be difficult when the time came to pay the settlement proceeds.

"You know he has the money, no secret there. But he's Vince Smith. Who knows what hoops he'll make you jump through to get paid?" Michael speculated.

"He'll do the right thing, eventually. Besides, Kolber will see to it. And he still has a profitable company. Bankruptcy, voluntary or involuntary, would disrupt things. Thanks for your understanding about the intrusion," Andrea replied.

"What happened to your nap?"

"I had to call Longbow and give him the news. He was so excited."

"I'm glad."

"Then, I called Zack to coordinate the settlement docs on the MDL—no rest for the weary or the recently traumatized.

"Take better care of yourself," Michael lectured. "I don't want to add to your trauma, but as long as you're not asleep, can we talk about the M thing?"

"I know I said the office, Michael, but let's wait until tonight so we aren't interrupted."

"Sounds like a plan. Your place or mine?"

"Your choice."

"Yours. I'll bring carry-out."

While Andrea straightened her apartment that evening, there was a knock on the door. Andrea opened it, and Michael stood at the threshold, holding a dozen long-stemmed roses and a carry-out bag from *The Meltdown*. The diner's greasy spoon odor dominated the roses' pleasant aroma. Andrea held the roses an inch from her nose and sniffed.

"They're beautiful, Michael. And you know how I feel about *The Meltdown*. This is wonderful. Thank you."

"Only the finest for you," he quipped, holding the bag of greasy burgers and onion rings to his face.

"Let me put these in water." She walked into the kitchen, pulled a glass pitcher out of the cupboard, and filled it halfway with water before dropping the flowers into the pitcher. She walked to the dining area, placed the flowers in the middle of the table, then returned to the living room.

"Wow. It smells divine in here, just like the greasy spoon!"

"An oxymoron if I ever heard one. You know, we had our first date at *The Meltdown*."

"It was hardly a date. As I recall, you were on a reconnaissance mission, doing surveillance work on me."

"I'm so glad I did. It was love at first sight."

"Sure."

"You're such a buzzkill."

"Keep going."

"Do you want to talk first or eat first?"

"I'm starving. Let's eat if you don't mind."

"Whatever Lola wants, Lola gets."

"Huh? Who's Lola?" Andrea never saw *Damn Yankees*.

"It's a song in a musical. *Damn Yankees*. Do you like musicals?"

"I couldn't afford live theater. Until recently, I was broke, remember? I'm happy to be educated, though."

"You will *love* live theater. I'll check the schedule in Chelsea. Jeff Daniels has *The Purple Rose Theatre* over there."

"I said I couldn't *afford* it. I didn't say I was deaf, dumb, and blind. *Everyone* in this area knows about *The Purple Rose*."

"Excuuuuse me!" Michael did his best Steve Martin impression.

"Sorry, I was harsh."

"All in fun. Let's eat."

They ate in relative silence, enjoying food and each other's company, uttering an occasional salute to the delicious garbage served at *The Meltdown*. Andrea poured two glasses of fruit punch when they finished eating. They adjourned to the couch. Michael offered a toast.

"To your continued health and success." He held up his glass. "May you have no more mornings like today."

"Amen to that." Andrea clinked her glass to his, and they took sips. Andrea grimaced.

"This is awful."

"But vital to my sobriety," Michael cautioned. "Can we talk?"

"You can always talk to me," she deflected.

"You know what I mean. Stop evading the issue."

"The floor is yours."

Michael rose from the couch, pulled out a ring box, and kneeled before her. He opened the box, revealing a three-carat solitaire diamond ring. Andrea was stunned. She expected a *conversation*, not a *proposal*.

"Andrea Kramer? Would you please make me the happiest man in the world? Please be my wife. Will you? Will you marry me?"

Andrea hesitated for a moment. Every good thing this year occurred *after* she met Michael O'Hara. He celebrated with her when she defeated him *twice* in court. She felt safe in his arms and loved every moment she spent with him. He loved her with all his heart, and she loved him. *What is there to think about?*

"Yes, Michael, *yes*. I will marry you! He took the ring from the case and placed it on her ring finger. *Too big*. She removed the ring, put it on her middle finger, and pointed it at him.

"That's my Andrea! I give you an engagement ring. You give me the finger."

"Whoops!" She didn't realize what she had done. She laughed, a wonderful, contagious laugh that caused Michael to crack up.

Andrea rose from the couch and knelt where Michael was still kneeling, holding the empty ring box. She leaned forward and kissed him, their first kiss as an engaged couple. They spent the rest of the night talking, making love, and enjoying each other's company.

***

Zachary Blake arrived at the office to surprise Andrea with the MDL settlement paperwork. While delighted to see him, she wondered why he suddenly appeared at the Haunted Barn. Zack suggested she call Michael into the conference room. Andrea pulled Michael out of his office for an emergency meeting.

"What's going on?" Michael came running into the conference room. Zack was sitting at the head of the table, sipping on a cup of coffee.

"Hey, Zack. What brings you here?"

"Hey, Michael. I brought the MDL settlement docs."

"Very sneaky, you two," Andrea folded her arms and stink-eyed the two of them.

"What?" Michael continued to feign innocence.

"Don't blame him," Zack urged. "Call it an engagement gift, Andrea. It was my idea. I didn't want you newly engaged people bickering over the settlement details. I called Michael to congratulate him on his engagement. Congrats to you, too, by the way."

"Thank you. Continue, please?"

"I told Michael what a lucky man he was. 'This woman is going places,' I told him. 'Sit back and enjoy the ride.'"

"And I said I couldn't speak for you. You liked things done a certain way. I *defended* you, Andrea," Michael pleaded his case.

"And I said, 'We'll tell her after I finish the paperwork.' So, here I am." Zack held up the documents. "See, the paperwork's done," Zack rested his case. "Hey! What is this? A cross-examination? I'm not saying another word without my attorney!"

Andrea laughed. "This is all very sweet and a great story, but a heads-up would have been nice."

"And what would you have said?" Michael challenged.

"Point taken. No bickering," she conceded.

Zack and Michael explained the entire package to Andrea. After his presentation, Zack handed her a flash drive with all the settlement templates and detailed how-to instructions. He even got the contingency fee portion of the settlement approved by Judge Kolber.

"It's wonderful to be King, isn't it, Zack?" Andrea chuckled.

"It has its perks. We *earned* these fees. Don't you agree, Michael?"

"Having been on the opposite side of you two, I agree. I'm pleased I can put away my slingshot."

Andrea wanted to be angry at their presumptuous behavior, but their hearts were in the right place. She was grateful for Zack's mentoring friendship and pleased to avoid bickering with Michael over final settlement details. When the meeting concluded, Zack rose to leave. He motioned Andrea over.

"Hug?" He opened his welcoming arms. The two lawyers embraced.

"Absolutely. Thank you for *everything*: the crash course in MDL, the cost float, your valuable advice, counsel, and mentoring. I'm so grateful."

"Stay in touch. My offer to join the Blake firm as a partner still stands."

Andrea glanced at Michael. "Thanks Zack. I appreciate your offer more than you know, but Michael and I have other plans. Besides, I like my little haunted house and barn. Didn't Michael do a fabulous job fixing this place up?"

"I didn't see it before, but it's beautiful now. Good luck to both of you. I hope we'll work together again soon."

Zack started for the door.

"Oh! I almost forgot." He pulled an envelope from his lapel pocket and handed it to Andrea. She opened the envelope and gasped. While she knew the checks were being cut, seeing the numbers in writing was incredibly satisfying. The Longbow settlement, large though it was, paled in comparison. Her share of the attorney fee was more than generous. Andrea Kramer suddenly became a *very* wealthy woman.

Zack wasn't done being kind to her in appreciation for all she did to enhance the MDL result.

"If you look at the accounting on the document enclosed with the checks, you will see a detailed spreadsheet listing all your client class members and their grid share of the proceeds. You have little to do here besides writing and presenting checks to satisfied clients. Any questions?"

"Oh my God, Zack! This is like the best engagement present ever!"

"Nonsense, Andrea. I agree the timing makes it seem so, but you worked extremely hard for these results. This is no present. If anyone deserves this, it is you. Take care of this money and use it wisely. I feel obligated to tell you that I once took my fame and fortune for granted. My hubris and arrogance caused me to go broke. Fame can be fleeting. I learned that lesson the hard way. I don't want you ever to be a comeback story. Promise me."

"I promise, Zack. Thanks for everything."

"Michael, you are a true professional and a pleasure to work with. Everything changed when you took the lead. You two are fortunate to have each other."

"High praise coming from you. Thank you," Michael replied. "It's always a pleasure working with you."

"Amen to that. From the bottom of my heart, thank you, thank you, *thank you*," Andrea added.

"You're quite welcome. I hope to see you soon."

"You will. Besides, we've got to get together. You promised to introduce me to your family."

"I did, didn't I? I'll talk to the boss and put you together. Bye now." The King of Justice walked out the door.

CHAPTER TWENTY-NINE

THE WEDDING

Andrea

The marriage of Andrea Kramer and Michael O'Hara was to be a small, catered affair at *Greenfield Village* in Dearborn. The couple initially planned a small wedding. They decided to involve their parents and immediately lost control of the process. They didn't care. It made their parents happy and allowed four happy people to get to know each other.

Michael looked handsome in a standard black tuxedo. He walked down the aisle with a parent on each arm. A vocalist sang Olivia Newton-John's "I Honestly Love You."

The music stopped, and a pianist played the traditional wedding song. Andrea appeared at the back of the chapel. She trembled slightly as her father and mother left their seats to retrieve her. She adored her white handmade crystal beaded tulle royal ball gown wedding dress with a chapel train. When her father reached her, he lifted her veil and kissed her on both cheeks.

"You look beautiful, sweetheart. Look at the stunning woman my little girl has become." He stepped back to admire her. "Michael is a fortunate man."

Dad stepped aside, and Mom repeated the tribute.

"My beautiful baby," she cried, wiping tears with a tissue.

After carefully replacing the veil, her parents assumed their places opposite Andrea, locked arms with her, and walked their precious daughter down the aisle. Andrea struggled to hold back tears of joy and appreciation.

Judges Alvin Rubin and Daniel Kolber performed the unique, non-religious ceremony in the *Mary-Martha Chapel* at *Greenfield Village*. Soft music played in the background as Judge Rubin stepped to the podium to give the invocation.

"Dear family and friends. Thank you for joining us for this beautiful occasion. Andrea Kramer and Michael O'Hara have pledged their undying love for each other and are here today to unite in marriage.

"This is not the beginning of their relationship by any means. This couple has spent months together, getting to know each other as friends, partners, and lovers, and we now bear witness to how their relationship has matured and grown. This ceremony is the ultimate affirmation of their bond.

"Andrea and Michael mark their union as a couple not only by celebrating *their* love but also the love between all of us. Without *your* love, dear friends and family, today would be far less joyous. Dan?"

Rubin invited Judge Kolber to take over at the podium. Kolber walked up and stood next to Judge Rubin.

"I echo the words of Judge Rubin. Having met and worked with this couple, seeing them in good times and bad, I have little doubt that this is a solid relationship built on mutual respect, devotion, admiration, and love. And now, Michael, Andrea, are you ready to take your vows?"

The couple faced each other and nodded.

"Michael," Kolber continued. "Do you take Andrea to be your lawfully wedded wife, to have, to hold, in sickness and health, in good times and bad, for richer or poorer, forsaking all others, for as long as you both shall live?"

Michael faced Andrea, holding both her hands in his. Tears ran down his face. She could not love him more than she did at this moment.

"I do."

"Andrea. Do you take Michael—"

"Yes!" Andrea blurted.

"Please allow me to finish your vows, young lady," Kolber scolded with a smile. Everyone in attendance laughed out loud.

"As I was saying, Andrea, do you take Michael to be your lawfully wedded husband, to have, to hold, in sickness and health, in good times and bad, for richer or poorer, forsaking all others, for as long as you both shall live?"

"I do," she repeated, slightly embarrassed.

"Alvin, the rings?"

Kolber stepped back, and Rubin stepped forward.

"Uh . . . Yes, Dan," he paused, patting himself down. "What did I do with those rings?" he jested. The guests gasped. "Oh! Here they are!" Rubin miraculously found them just in time to continue. Andrea was not amused. Rubin continued the ceremony.

"Andrea and Michael have chosen rings to exchange with each other as a symbol of their undying love. Michael, as you place this ring on Andrea's finger, please repeat after me. With this ring, I thee wed and pledge you my love, now and forever."

Michael repeated the words with tears in his eyes.

"Andrea, and don't interrupt me, young lady!" The attendees laughed this time. Judge Rubin called for quiet, and the crowd settled down.

"As you place this ring on Michael's finger, please repeat after me. With this ring, I thee wed and pledge you my love, now and forever."

Andrea repeated the words with love in her heart.

The two judges stood side by side and spoke in unison.

"By the authority vested in us by the state of Michigan, we now pronounce you husband and wife. Michael, Andrea, you may kiss your spouse."

The couple kissed, and the audience whooped. Andrea was overwhelmed with joy. The soft music that played throughout the ceremony became loud and celebratory. The couple dashed down the aisle, confetti thrown at them from all angles.

Outside the chapel, a horse-drawn carriage awaited them. With the help of friends and family, the couple climbed into the carriage and was transported to the *Eagle Tavern* in the heart of the village. The tavern was built in 1850, with a unique front porch, hardwood floors, and historic tables and chairs. An elegant ice sculpture stood at the head of the room, courtesy of Michael's parents. Warm candlelight and fireplaces dotted the intimate space, creating a memorable atmosphere.

Dinner was fabulous—multiple toasts were made, keeping the guests laughing joyfully throughout the evening. A classic band played standards for guests and the happy couple to dance to.

Instead of dessert, there was a giant wedding cake and a chocolate fountain, gifts from Michael's parents. The photographer called the happy couple to the dance floor to cut the cake. They took turns stuffing cake in each other's faces, creating a mess. The caterer brought them wet towels to clean their faces. Of course, everyone laughed at the sight.

At the end of a fabulous evening, Andrea and Michael said farewell, thanked their guests, and thanked their parents for their love and support. They climbed into the carriage once more, and the driver took them to the front gate, where a limousine waited to transport them to *The Henry*, a beautiful boutique hotel near the village. The honeymoon suite was reserved in their name.

The clerk checked them in, and a bellhop escorted them to the suite. The hotel had prepared for their arrival with flowers, candles, champagne, and snacks. Soft music played in the background. A beautiful jacuzzi tub was built into the floor. Michael helped unfasten her wedding dress, and she slipped into the bathroom to freshen up. Michael walked to the jacuzzi, turned on the faucet, and tested the water. When he had the perfect mixture of hot and cold, he plugged the drain, and the tub began to fill.

Michael placed some candles around the room, including a couple on the floor near the jacuzzi. He opened a box of cherry cordials and put them on the lip of the tub.

The bathroom door opened. Andrea stood before him. Candlelight flames danced on her body.

"My God!" Michael gasped.

"What?"

"You are so beautiful! I am the luckiest man alive!"

"You're not so bad yourself. I like what you've done with the room, but you forgot something."

Michael looked around. It was perfect. *What's missing?* He shrugged, looking disappointed. "Looks pretty inviting to me. What did I miss?"

"You still have your clothes on."

"Shit!"

Michael jumped to his feet, pulled off his tuxedo jacket, and began fumbling with the silver tuxedo buttons, having difficulty removing them in his slightly altered state. Andrea walked over to him, brushed his lips with a kiss, and slowly removed each button until the shirt was open. She reached up and pulled the suspenders off his shoulders—they fell to the sides of his trousers. Gently, she grabbed each side of the shirt, reached around him, and pulled the shirt off his body, tossing it on the floor.

Next, she unfastened his trousers and slowly pushed them down, bending down with them as she gently lowered them to the ground. Michael bent over and rubbed her bare back as she completed the task, and he stepped out of the trousers. She lifted his feet, one at a time, and removed his socks. Then, she started her way back up, grabbing the waistband of his boxers and pulling them down.

Andrea took Michael by the hand. They stepped down into the warm waters of the jacuzzi tub. She could see the happiness and love in his eyes, feel it in her heart. She once wondered what true love would be like. Would it ever happen? Yet, here she was, married to a man she could not love more, beginning a new life, personally and professionally, with her partner and lover, her *husband*, Michael O'Hara. She had never known joy like this.

They sat in the tub, facing each other. Michael reached around his bride and turned on the jacuzzi jets; the vibrations caused the candles to dance around the tub, creating the perfect mood. They moved slowly toward each other until they came together, drunk with love, desperate to hold each other and make love for the first time as man and wife.

"I love you," Michael whispered as he began to kiss her *everywhere.*

"Ditto," she giggled.

Michael stopped what he was doing and studied her.

"Ditto?" He pouted.

"See? Not very romantic, is it?"

He stuck out his already protruding lower lip in another of his exaggerated pouts.

"Oh, stop your annoying pouting, you big baby!" she scolded. "I love you, too."

His expression immediately changed, and he resumed kissing every part of her, taking in the taste and smell of the woman he loved.

They made love that evening, as man and wife, in the jacuzzi, in the bed, on the floor, on the couch, anywhere in the hotel room where love was possible. And when they awoke in the morning, they made love again.

After room service brought an elaborate breakfast spread, they dressed casually and headed to the lobby. The hotel had already checked them out, and a limousine awaited their arrival at the front entrance to take them to the airport. Their packed bags were in the trunk of the limo. Their parents had thought of everything!

They drank coffee and made out in the back seat of the limo. They might have made love again if the airport hadn't been close to the hotel. The driver pulled up at the *McNamara Terminal* at *Detroit Metropolitan Airport.*

To their great surprise, their parents and other wedding guests stood at the entrance to the terminal, tossing flower petals and confetti as they walked into the terminal. A photographer and videographer captured the entire event. The group spent some time celebrating inside the terminal at the lower level until it was time for the bride and groom to head for the gate.

Andrea and Michael said goodbye to their parents, relatives, and friends an hour later. Finally, they headed to the gate, where a Delta jet was preparing to take them to the Greek Isles for a fabulous honeymoon.

EPILOGUE

THE PARTNERSHIP

Andrea

Andrea and Michael O'Hara had a fabulous time on their honeymoon. Greece and the Greek Islands were splendid destinations, made even more pleasurable by the couple's newfound wealth. They spared no expense and booked what the touring company called a 10-day romance luxury tour of Athens, Mykonos, and Santorini.

After an unforgettable honeymoon experience, returning to the mundane tasks of managing a law office and practicing law was difficult. They contacted their landlord, made him an offer he couldn't refuse, and purchased the haunted office and barn. After the closing, they expanded the old building to accommodate more attorneys and staff and make it more client friendly.

Keeping their relationship professional at the office was even more difficult than purchasing and renovating the building. They wanted to make love every time their paths crossed at the office.

Sometimes, at lunchtime, they would leave the office at separate times only to rush to the apartment for an afternoon delight. They were fooling no one, as everyone in the office knew where they went and what they did when they arrived.

The criminal case against Michigan Watch Patrol members was resolved with multiple guilty pleas. The original four men arrested turned State's evidence on several more members. To avoid a felony murder charge, Brandon North pleaded guilty to manslaughter. His co-defendants pleaded guilty to murder in the second degree.

After a whirlwind of activity, the conclusion of Andrea's two huge cases and the criminal case, Michael's hourly fee windfall, the Emma Simpson case, their courtship, engagement, wedding, honeymoon, and the renovation and purchase of their building, Andrea and Michael sat in their apartment reflecting on their good fortune.

Andrea announced she had a surprise for Michael.

"But I have everything a man could want," he protested.

"We are true partners in life, right?" she inquired.

"Right," he conceded with a puzzled look on his face.

"So, life partners—law partners." Andrea walked to the closet and pulled out a dynamic outdoor sign:

O'HARA & O'HARA PLLC
ATTORNEYS AT LAW

Andrea Kramer O'Hara
Michael O'Hara

Partners

"This is wonderful. Are you sure?" Michael gasped.
"I've never been surer of anything in my life," she assured him.
"I won't let you down." He held the sign out in front of his face.

"What a beautiful sign! Let's head to the office and hang it!"

"Now? It's almost time for bed. Do you want to? Or would you rather hop into bed, *have your way with me*, go to sleep, and hang the sign in the morning?" She gave him the eye waggle.

Michael grabbed the sign and returned it to the closet. He turned back and shouted:

"What are you waiting for? Quick, to the bedroom!"

THE END

About the Author

Mark M. Bello is an attorney, social justice advocate, and award-winning author of the Zachary Blake Legal Thriller series. Mark also writes for legal and political content sites and hosts the legal-themed podcast, *Justice Counts*, on the *Spreaker* network. A Michigan native, Mark and his wife, Tobye, have four children and nine grandchildren. For more information, please visit *https://www.markmbello.com*.

Previous Books

in the Zachary

Blake Legal Thriller Series

L'DOR V'DOR –From Generation to Generation

(A Prequel Novella)

Betrayal of Faith (1)

Betrayal of Justice (2)

Betrayal in Blue (3)

Betrayal in Black (4)

Betrayal High (5)

Supreme Betrayal (6)

Betrayal at the Border (7)

You Have the Right to Remain Silent (8)

The Zachary Blake Legal Thriller Series

is also available in audiobook format.

Books in the Harbor Springs Cozy Legal Mystery Series

The Final Steps (1)

Books in Mark's Social Justice/Safety Series for Children

HAPPY JACK SAD JACK— A Bullying Story (1)

ONE THING OR TWO— ASHER'S DISTRACTED LESSON (2)

Other Books by Mark M. Bello

L'DOR V'DOR-From Generation to Generation, a Holocaust Era
Novella

L'DOR V'DOR –From Generation to Generation II

The Blake-Lewin Family Cookbook of Traditional Jewish Recipes

Connect with Mark

Website: https://www.markmbello.com

Email: info@markmbello.com

Facebook: MarkMBelloBooks

Twitter: @MarkMBelloBooks

YouTube: Mark Bello

Goodreads: Mark M. Bello

LinkedIn:

https://www.linkedin.com/in/markmbello

Subscribe to our mailing list and receive your *free copy* of

L'DOR V'DOR -From Generation to Generation

and other giveaways and other surprises.

To request a speaking engagement, interview, or appearance,
please email info@markmbello.com

www.ingramcontent.com/pod-product-compliance
Lightning Source LLC
Chambersburg PA
CBHW020752190726

48285CB00006B/1991